SECRETLY
WAITING

SECRETLY
WAITING

CYNTHIA LEBRON

XULON ELITE

Xulon Press Elite
2301 Lucien Way #415
Maitland, FL 32751
407.339.4217
www.xulonpress.com

© 2023 by Cynthia Lebron

Contribution by: My Lord JESUS CHRIST

All rights reserved solely by the author. The author guarantees all contents are original and do not infringe upon the legal rights of any other person or work. No part of this book may be reproduced in any form without the permission of the author. The views expressed in this book are not necessarily those of the publisher.

Due to the changing nature of the Internet, if there are any web addresses, links, or URLs included in this manuscript, these may have been altered and may no longer be accessible. The views and opinions shared in this book belong solely to the author and do not necessarily reflect those of the publisher. The publisher, therefore, disclaims responsibility for the views or opinions expressed within the work.

Unless otherwise indicated, Scripture quotations taken from the King James Version (KJV) – *public domain*.

Paperback ISBN-13: 978-1-66286-825-2
Ebook ISBN-13: 978-1-66286-826-9

I dedicate this book to:

My Lord & Savior JESUS CHRIST

My fine husband:
William Lebron III

Our amazing children:
Lelani
Philip
Samantha
Will
Adonijah

Our beautiful granddaughter:
Aleia

WILLIAM &. CYNTHIA. LEBRON

OUR CHILDREN

Contents

Chapter 1 The Encounter 1

Chapter 2 Birthday Bash 7

Chapter 3 Deceptions 21

Chapter 4 Confrontations 39

Chapter 5 Mission Trip 55

Chapter 6 Broken 67

Chapter 7 Graduation Cruise 77

Chapter 8 The Wedding 87

Chapter 1: The Encounter

Today's the big day; I'm seventeen now. I run downstairs and see my parents surprise me with my first car. All my friends and family are here to celebrate with me. As a seventeen-year-old kid, I have everything I could ever want, but the truth is I have a deep desire that my friends and family don't even know about. I desire for my Lord God to show me who I will marry in the future, and I believe God will . . .

One night when I was fourteen years old, around 3 a.m., I couldn't sleep. I woke up because I heard a noise. "Who's there?" I said as I looked around the room carefully. Then there was a light coming from the corner on the other side of the room. "Who are you?" I asked. Then a soft voice came from the light and said, "I am the Angel of the Lord. Your request has been granted. At the age of seventeen, you will see your future wife, but you must not speak to her or make her notice you until the appointed time; so you know, her name has an L in it. When you're eighteen years old, you'll both meet and become friends, but you won't get married until you're twenty years old. You must not tell her or anyone else about this encounter until after you're married to her." Then He was gone.

When I woke up in the morning, I wondered if I was dreaming or if that really happened, but since then, I've waited for my seventeenth birthday with the hope of finally knowing who she is.

I want to know her, see her grow up as I grow up, see the choices she makes, friends she has, how she takes care of herself and prepares herself for me, her future husband. That's why today is so important to me because any day soon, I can know who she is.

Days go by. I feel excited and anxious every morning, wondering if this day will be the day. Then days turn into weeks and weeks into months. I begin feeling hopeless like maybe it's not going to happen, and I need to move on . . . so I do.

Nine months later . . .

Today, I'm helping my girlfriend prepare for tonight's homecoming celebration. She's practically got the whole school to come. She's really excited about it because it's our first homecoming together. I know what you're thinking; is she the one? Well . . . I've known her since the second grade, and even though I never wanted to date anyone else but the one I'm supposed to marry, I'm tired of waiting around . . . so I guess my feelings have changed. Plus, I really like her, so I'm hoping she is the one. She came up to me two months ago at youth group night and let me know how much she likes me. I thought she looked good, so I asked her out, and here we are. These past two months have been great having my first girlfriend, and she loves God. We go to the same church, and our parents are good friends. I think she's perfect for me.

One night we went out alone, and things got a little intense, and I came close to breaking my promise to God. I felt so ashamed because I'm saving myself for marriage and want to honor God. We told each other we won't let that happen again, but honestly, part of me kind of wants it to happen again because maybe she is the one, and I didn't realize it. I'm about to be eighteen years old in three months, and I'm thinking about asking her to marry me. Or maybe I'm letting my feelings get the best of me, and I'm not thinking straight.

Chapter 1: The Encounter

Anyways . . .

The party is poppin.' Everybody came, even people I don't know! The party's almost over, and everybody's still here. As I walk into the kitchen to grab some snacks, I look over at the window and see a glistening like if the window was broken. As I get closer to check it out, my heart starts beating like a hundred beats per second. I feel my body temperature rising and am extremely nervous and excited! I don't know what to do right now. I think it's her, the one God told me about since I was fourteen. Even though I never met her before, I just feel like it's her.

As I look back out the window, I see her talking with a guy and some other girls. I think, "Wow, she is beautiful!" I can't help but wonder if that guy is her boyfriend.

Suddenly, I jump when I hear Jennifer call my name as she walks into the kitchen.

"There you are," she says. "I've been looking everywhere for you."

"Well, you found me," I say jokingly, even though I feel super nervous.

"You're so funny, JR!"

"Wow, Jen, there's a lot of people here at your party, even some I've never seen before."

"Yeah, I invited everyone; sorry I didn't get to introduce you to them all."

"It's ok. You can just stand next to me by the window, point them all out, and tell me their names because I can always meet everyone at your next party," I sarcastically respond.

Jen laughs, then starts pointing everyone out while explaining a little about each of them and how she knows them. Finally, she gets to the group I've been waiting for.

"Ok, that's Tony; he's new to our school. He's in one of my classes and on the football team.

"That's Liza, and she just moved to South Florida a week and a half ago from New York. I met her at the gym, where she works part-time making protein shakes. She was so cool that we instantly became friends.

"That's Jael; she's also from New York, and she's Liza's cousin. She's really smart and skipped a grade so she's in college a year early.

"And that's Daisy, a girl from school who I don't really know that well, but she's in one of my classes."

"I look forward to meeting all your friends soon, Jen, but I'm kind of tired, so I'm going to start cleaning up and head home."

"Ok, JR. Thanks!"

The night ends, and I've been thinking a lot about what just happened. I feel a little torn because I was hoping that Jen was the one, but I really believe Liza is the one God told me about, and as I think about her, I get overwhelmingly excited of what my life would be like with her. I'm so messed up right now because if Jen did that to me, I'd be mad upset.

My God, help me recognize what your will is for me to do right now.

As I walk down the hallways at school, I look everywhere to see if I can see Liza without being obvious. There she is . . . standing in the lunchroom, talking to that guy from the party. He's hugging up all over her, and she's not stopping him.

"Hi, JR . . . are you ready for lunch?" Jen asks.

"Yeah, I'm starving. So Jen, your friend Liza . . . she's making friends pretty quickly, huh?"

"Yeah, she is, and ever since the party where her and Tony met, they started dating."

"Wow, that's great, but isn't it kind of weird that she just met him, and now they're dating?"

"No, they really like each other."

"Ok, if you say so." I say very passively.

"Why do you even care, JR?" She scoffs.

Oh no, I think I'm being obvious. I need to redirect the conversation.

"I just care about the type of friends you have because you're my girl." I say convincingly.

"Don't worry. She's not that type of girl."

"Alright, cool."

Huh, that was a close one, but now every time I see Liza with her boyfriend, I feel crazy jealous and think back to that night when God told me about her. Why is she kissing that guy, hugging up on him, and probably falling for him? Why?

I feel like a stalker. I know Liza's schedule, where she lives, and who she hangs out with. I even watch her from behind trees.

Help me, Lord; this isn't like me.

Two and a half months later . . .

While at dinner with Jen, the conversation gets interesting.

"JR, why don't you let me help you plan your eighteenth birthday bash?

"I would be honored, Jen!"

"Yay! By the way, there's something I've been wanting to tell you."

"What is it?" I asked curiously.

"I love you, JR, and I've been thinking about taking our relationship to the next level."

"I love you too, Jen, but what do you mean by 'next level?'"

"Well . . . we graduate high school in a few months, you're about to be eighteen in less than two weeks, and I will be eighteen four months after you. We've already talked about getting married one day, and I think that we should sleep together."

"Wow, Jen." I said as I spit out my drink. "I've thought about that too, but it's wrong before marriage in God's eyes."

"I don't think it's wrong since we're going to get married soon."

"We haven't really decided about getting married yet, Jen. We only spoke about it. We really need to pray about it because we're still very young."

"I'm so happy you feel the same way, JR, and you're right; we should pray about it."

Lord I'm so confused, I feel tempted to sleep with Jen, but I know it's wrong, and I don't want to take a chance and lose Liza because I think that she's the one you spoke to me about when I was fourteen. But she doesn't even know me yet. Lord Jesus, please help me . . . I don't know what to do in this situation. I need time, Lord.

Chapter 2: Birthday Bash

It's December 1st and it's my birthday. I'm so excited about my birthday bash that I couldn't sleep last night! This is going to be the best bash ever . . . Everyone's coming, even Liza and her boyfriend. I'm just going to have fun, but in the back of my mind, I know that at eighteen years old, we're supposed to meet and become friends. So I'm going to try to do that tonight!

"Wow, Jen! You look slammin' in that dress!"
"Thanks, JR. You don't look so bad yourself! So . . . my parents went away for the weekend, and I'll be home all by myself. I would love it if you came over to keep me company."
Her invitation catches me off guard, but I try to play it off.
"I would love to, Jen, but I'm not sure if I can."
"Think about it, but for now, let's dance!" she says as she pulls me in to dance.

I'm really trying to enjoy myself with Jen, but I can't seem to shake our previous conversation. Is she trying to set me up? How can she say it so casually? I think she's just trying to get me alone and I'm not falling for it.

"We've been dancing for about thirty minutes straight. I need a break." I say almost breathless.

"All right, all right. You get tired so quickly for an eighteen-year-old."

She grabs my hand to make our way back to the seats. Suddenly I notice her lock eyes with Liza.

"Oh, there's Liza, Jael, and Tony. I'm going to call them over here so I can finally introduce you to them." she speaks.
"Ok!" I say full of nervous excitement.

"Liza, Jael, Tony, this is JR, my boyfriend."
"Nice to meet you, JR!" They say collectively.
"It's nice to meet you guys too. Would you like to come chill with us?" I say trying to sound as cool as possible.
"Sure, that's cool." says Tony.

We all make our way over to the lounge area.

"So Tony, where you from?" I ask as if I don't already know, and it's not like I really care about where he's from anyway.
"I'm from here, South Florida. I just moved to this neighborhood and started coming to our school in August."
"How 'bout you, Liza?" I ask trying to compose myself from the excitement.
"My cousin Jael and I moved to South Florida from New York in August. We really love it here. So, tell us about you, JR?"

"I'm also from NY but moved to South Florida when I was little, and I love it here too." I say confidently.
"So maybe we should all hang out sometime and get to know each other better," Jen says.
"That sounds great!" they all say.
I can't believe that this is really happening just like the Lord said, on my eighteenth birthday. I can't wait to hang out with Liza.
"It's time for the cake and to sing to the birthday boy!" says Jen.

CHAPTER 2: BIRTHDAY BASH

"Happy birthday to you, happy birthday to you, happy birthday Josiah, happy birthday to you! Yay!"

"I'm going to start serving the cake; wait here, and I'll bring you your piece, JR." Jen says.
"Yes, please! I can't wait to taste it!" I say as I anxiously wait for my favorite cake (strawberry peach sensation).

"Happy birthday, JR. I didn't know your name is Josiah," says Liza as she walks up to me.
"Yeah, my parents named me after King Josiah in the Bible."
"Wow, that's so cool."
"Your name is really cool too!" I say blushing.
"Well, my name is Elisheba, after Aaron's wife in the Bible, but everybody calls me Liza."

"Wow, I like your real name too!"
"Thanks, JR!"
"So, where's Tony?" I ask
"He went to the bathroom." She
"Oh ok. By the way, you look very beautiful tonight!" I say discreetly.
"Oh stop! You're making me blush!"
"So you and Tony are pretty serious, huh?"
"Well . . . I don't know. We've only been dating for a little while. We don't even see each other besides at school and parties. My parents don't even know we're dating because I'm not allowed to date, and to tell you the truth, I really like him, but part of me feels like . . . Wow. I'm so sorry. I shouldn't be talking about this." She says as she puts down her drink.
"No, I'm sorry for getting into your personal business," I say with concern.
"It's ok. Excuse me, I got to go get some cake."

"Yeah, go ahead. See you around."

Lord I'm such an idiot. Why did I ask about her and Tony right now? I mean . . . I should have waited until we got to know each other better. Lord, please give me the wisdom I need to know what to say and what not to say.

"Here's your piece of cake." says Jen.

"Thank you, Jen. I want to know what you think about inviting Tony, Liza, and Jael to youth group on Wednesday night?"
"Yeah, we should. I'm going to go ask them now." she says as she starts walking towards them.

I really hope Liza agrees to come to youth group. Here comes Jen with their response.

"So . . . what did they say?" I ask anxiously.
"They'll be there."
"That's great, Jen!"

"When you drive me home tonight, I would like for you to sleep over."

I can't believe Jen is trying to get to sleep over.

"Where would I sleep?" I ask.
"You can sleep on the couch."
"I'll think about it, Jen."
"Ok!"

While at Jen's house, I'm feeling a little nervous. I don't want to do something stupid.

Chapter 2: Birthday Bash

"I don't feel right about being alone with you without your parents knowing."

"It's fine, JR. We're in love and planning on getting married. Just kiss me and don't think about anything else."

"Ok, Jen."

"What are you doing, Jen?" I ask as I try pushing her off me.

"Relax, JR. this is called foreplay."

"Get off me, Jen. I gotta go!"

"Okay, JR. I'm sorry."

This girl is crazy Lord, she's trying to get me to sin against you. I'm so glad I left when I did.

Finally made it to youth tonight. I'm hoping to see Liza here.

"I'm so excited you girls made it tonight, but where's Tony?" Jen asks.

"He didn't want to come; he said he's not really into church stuff." Liza replies.

Jen shows Liza and Jael around the church and introduces them.

"Hi, Liza!" I say anxiously.

"Hi, JR," she awkwardly says.

"What's that all about, JR?" asks Jen.

"Oh nothing, she's probably nervous because it's her first time here."

Oh no, Lord! She hates me now. I got to do something about this. I can't let this be the end of me getting to know her. Lord, give me an opportunity to fix this.

"Everyone, gather around. The service is about to start. Tonight, we're going to talk about God's love for us and how He loves us so much that He'd rather die than to live without us . . . and He did!" says the youth pastor."

"Wow, youth service was amazing! I felt so convicted, uplifted, and loved all at the same time," Liza describes as she wipes away tears of joy after going up to the altar and confessing Jesus Christ as her Lord and Savior. "Thank you guys so much for inviting us!"

"Anytime. How 'bout you, Jael? How'd you like it?" I ask.

"It was great, JR. He really preached the truth with such passion! I'm excited to see what the Lord has in store through this ministry."

"It sounds like you've already given your life to Christ, Jael."

"I did when I was thirteen years old." she replied.

"Wow, that's awesome, Jael."

"Thanks, JR. See you guys next week."

"You're welcome, and we look forward to it!"

It truly was an amazing night to see Liza so bold and excited about giving her life to You, Jesus. I guess I always pictured my future wife to be raised in church and already know You Lord, but it also stirred a little godly jealousy in me. I need to get closer to You, Lord Jesus, and have that excitement for You like I did when I was younger.

Today, I'm running errands with my mom, and I've been thinking about Liza and how awkward she feels around me ever since the party.

"Hey, Josiah!"

"Hey Liza, what's up?"

Chapter 2: Birthday Bash

"I'm here shopping with my parents. By the way, this is my dad David and my mom Abigail. Mom, Dad, this is Josiah, a friend from school!" she says.

"So nice to meet you! I'm Josiah, and this is my mom Sofia!"

"It's a pleasure to meet you! Are you guys new to the area?" my mom asks Liza's parents.

"Yes, we are." says her mom.

"Well, I would like to invite your family to come over to our house next Saturday so we can welcome you to the neighborhood and get to know each other," my mom says.

"Sounds great! We'll be there with the dessert." says Liza's dad.

As our parents continued talking, Liza and I got to conversate a little.

"It's so cool that are our parents kind of hit it off!" Liza expresses.

"Yeah, it is, but . . . ah . . . listen, Liza, I've been meaning to talk to you and apologize for the other night. I don't want you to feel awkward with me."

"It's not your fault. I just felt weird because I don't really share my feelings very often."

"Well, if you don't mind, I would like it if we can be friends, and I can be someone you trust with your feelings someday." I say trying to show her that I'm here for her.

"I would really like that too, Josiah"

"I'm going to need your number so I can text you my address."

"Oh, that's right."

Yes! I got her number! Woohoo! I've been waiting for this moment for a long time! I can't wait until next Saturday's dinner.

It's finally Saturday and I'm so excited to see Liza. She is so beautiful. When I'm around her, I don't even think about Jen.

"You have such a beautiful home, Josiah." Liza says admiringly.
"Thanks, Liza! Come, let me show you my favorite hangout spot."
"Ok!"
"All right, this is it." I say as I show her my favorite spot in my backyard.
"Wow, this is so cozy and beautiful!"

"Thanks! This is where I come to talk to God, share every thought and everything that happens in the day."
"That's so awesome, I need a spot like this at my house where no one bothers me, and it's just the Lord and me."
"You can have that in your house too."

"So Josiah, since you want us to become friends, let me ask you a question."
"Ok, shoot."
"How are things between you and Jen?"
"Well, ahh . . . things are going well." I say nervously.
"You didn't say that with much confidence; please trust that anything you tell me stays between us."
"Well . . . we've been dating since summer, and she wants to get married."
"Whoa, that's kind of sudden. So, do you love her and want to marry her?" Liza asks curiously.
"At one point, I thought I did, but now I'm not so sure."
"So, what changed?"
"Well, that's something that I can't share right now. I'm sorry, Liza."

CHAPTER 2: BIRTHDAY BASH

"I understand. The more you get to know me, the more you'll be open to sharing with me."

"Yeah, thanks for understanding. Now come on, let's go eat before our parents start wondering where we are."

"True. We don't want them to think anything."

This has been the most amazing night, Lord! Liza is so beautiful and down to earth. My heart was beating so fast the whole time I was with her. I tried to play it cool, and I think she digs me. I love that she calls me Josiah. I'm so looking forward to the next time I spend time with her.

It's New Year's Eve, and I get to spend it with my family and, best of all, Liza and her family! I'm wearing my best outfit and going to try to get a hug from her when the ball drops. I'm counting on you, Lord.

One hour left until the New Year and I'm hanging out with Liza.

"Have you noticed our parents love hanging out together, they've hung out every other day since they met at Walmart?" I point out.

"I think that's awesome!"

"Yeah, me too, Liza!"

"So what's your New Year's resolution, Josiah?"

"For the new year, I'm going to grow closer to my Lord Jesus Christ, and I'm going to make sure I work out so I can keep these big guns," I say laughing.

"You're so crazy, Josiah."

"How 'bout you, Liza?"

"Mine is also to grow closer to my Lord Jesus and focus on doing great in school so I can achieve everything God wants me to."

"That's great. You know . . . I can help you with your resolution by tutoring you in any classes you need extra help. I don't mean to brag, but I am a straight-A student." I sarcastically say.

"All right, and I can help you with yours by hooking you up with a gym membership where I work and being your workout partner."

"That's awesome Liza. Let's do it!"

"Ok, we can start tomorrow! Now hurry Josiah, take my hand and let's run to our parents. There's one minute left until the new year!"

"Five . . . four . . . three . . . two . . . one . . . Happy New Year!"

This has been another amazing night. Thank you, Lord! I got to hug my future wife tonight! She let me hold her hand for a whole twenty seconds. I think she might like me. Tomorrow, I get to work out with her and check her out at the same time!

I'm here at the gym with Liza, and she's making me workout like an athlete.

"That was a hard workout, but it hurts so good!" I say as I rub my sore arms.

"Let me make you the best protein shake you'll ever taste." she says.

"I'll be the judge of that, Liza Nuñez."

Suddenly I see Jen coming from the corner of my eye.

"JR, what are you doing here?" Jen asks.

"Hi, Jen. I just got a membership here and was working out."

"Oh, how come you didn't tell me?" she questions.

"I'm so sorry. It must have slipped my mind."

"It's ok; this is great news because we can be workout buddies!"

CHAPTER 2: BIRTHDAY BASH

"Sure, Jen . . . we can make it into a group workout. We'll have Tony and Liza work out with us." I suggest to her, even though I don't want that.

"Great idea, JR! Let me go talk to Liza."

Oh, my goodness, that was a close one. I totally forgot about Jen. I feel so confused right now. I love Jen, but I'm falling for Liza. I'm scared that Jen might think something is up. Help me, Jesus.

Jen is over there asking Liza about working out with us. I really want it to be just Liza and me. I can hear Jen speaking with her and I'm nervous.

"Hey Liza, JR and I want to know if you and Tony could be our workout buddies?"

"Yeah sure. I'll let Tony know." Liza says confused because she and I already agreed to be workout bubbies.

"So . . . Liza, we have so much to catch up on because you haven't been around here that much. What have you been doing?" Jen asks.

"Well, my parents became friends with Josiah's parents, and all they want to do is hang out at their house."

"Oh, that's nice; so, you've been hanging out there too?" questions Jen.

"Yeah, they make me go with them."

"So, what do you do for fun while you're there?" Jen asks as if she's interrogating Liza.

"Mainly talk with Josiah, and we all do family things together." Liza responds.

"Oh ok . . . so back to what I was saying . . . there's so much I've got to tell you. Like JR and I are getting married when school finishes. I'm so excited to spend the rest of my life with him!"

What? This is news to me. She expressed it to me, but I never agreed to marry her when school finishes. Why is lying to Liza? She must feel threatened by her. I know Liza won't believe her.

"Wow, congratulations, Jen! I had no idea."
"Thank you, Liza! So now that we're going to be hanging out at the gym, we'll have more time to catch up."
"Awesome." Liza awkwardly responds.

"Hey, JR. I just spoke with Liza, and she doesn't mind if all of us are workout partners."
"Oh . . . ok, great," I nervously answer without confronting what I just overheard.

I'm here at Liza's house to tutor her.
"All right, Liza, are you ready to get the best tutoring in math you've ever had?"
"Yes, Josiah . . . I am."
"What's wrong, Liza? I ask because she's acting cold.
"I'm ok. I just thought that we were going to tell each other everything, and you didn't tell me that you were going to marry Jen."

"Look, Liza, that's not how it happened. I did tell her I would pray about it, but that's all . . . I never said I would. Trust me . . . you're the coolest friend I have, and I wouldn't want to mess anything up between us." I say to reassure her.
"Thanks. That means a lot to me, Josiah, because I enjoy having you as my friend, and I feel like I can tell you anything." she says.

I love that she said that to me, I feel like she might have feelings for me.

Chapter 2: Birthday Bash

"Liza, can I ask you a question?"

"Sure, Josiah."

"Do you believe that God has a man for you to be with for the rest of your life?" I ask.

"I do . . . I even have dreams about it at times." she replies.

"Well, I do too, and that's why I don't want to marry just anyone; she has to be the one God has for me." I express.

"So why are you dating Jen if you're not sure if she's the one?" Liza asks. "Dating around isn't exactly waiting."

"Whoa, Liza, you have a point here, but I guess I got tired of waiting and wanted to be in a relationship, hoping that she might be the one." I answer reluctantly.

"Ok, but if she's not the one, you might be ruining your chances with the girl that is the one." she responds.

"Wow, I never thought of it that way."

"I never thought of it that way either, Josiah, until just now."

"I've got a lot of praying and thinking to do about this." I respond knowing that this could be true.

"Yeah, me too, but for right now, it's tutor time with Josiah Fernandez." she says trying to make me laugh.

Lord, I never thought that I would be ruining my chances with Liza because I was impatient and started dating Jen. At times, I think Liza's feeling me, but then she kind of seems like she just wants to be friends. Lord, I need direction on what to do with Jen. I'm convinced she's not the one, and Liza is. How should I break up with her without making it seem it's because of Liza, or maybe I can somehow make her break up with me so I won't have to make her feel bad? Lord, please help me outta this situation I put myself in. I want to tell Liza she's the one so bad, but I will wait on you, Lord.

Chapter 3: Deceptions

Three months later . . .

I'm on my way to school, thinking it's time to start preparing for prom. I've been trying to distance myself from Jen, but nothing is working. Liza and I have become the best of friends; she's amazing, and I'm falling for her so hard. I want to ask Liza to the prom without causing a problem with Jen or Tony; I don't know how yet, but I have a month to figure it out.

"Hi, JR. I want to introduce you to my new friend Aileen from school!" Jen exclaimed.

"Hi, Aileen . . . nice to meet you. I've seen you in my history class." I say to her.

"Yeah, that's me." says Aileen.

"Well, all right, ladies, I got to get to class. Talk to yah later." I say as I walk away.

"Bye, JR." they say.

Is it just me, or was that girl Aileen checkin' me out? I sense in my spirit that there's something suspect about that girl. I don't know what it is, but I know you'll reveal it to me soon, Lord.

"Wow, Jen . . . JR is fine, I didn't know he's your man." Aileen says obnoxiously.

"Yes, he is all mine, and hopefully soon-to-be husband." Jen defensively answers.

"Calm down, Jen. I didn't mean anything by it. By the way I'm still going to work out with you guys." Aileen says.

"You can work out with us right after school." Jen replies reluctantly.

We're all at the gym and supposed to workout together. Jen is there introducing everyone to her new friend Aileen. I can't wait for this to be over and get out of here.

"Hey guys, I invited my friend Aileen to workout with us. I hope you all don't mind." says Jen.

"That's fine." Liza says.

"So, you're Tony, the famous wide receiver on the football team." Aileen comments as she drools over his biceps.

"That's me!" He replies enjoying the attention.

I knew it; now Aileen is flirting with Tony. Even though I would love for her to steal Tony away from Liza, she's looking like a bad influence. She's a huge flirt, and I hope Jen doesn't become like that by hanging out with her.

Lord . . . You did say in the Bible that bad company corrupts good manners.

I'm surprised the workout went well. Now Aileen is inviting Jen to go to a pizza shop. I don't know if Jen should hang out with Aileen, but it's up to her.

When Jen and Aileen arrive at the pizza shop, two guys come up to them.

"Hey, Jen, this is my boyfriend Josh and his friend Joey from college." Aileen says with a huge smile on her face.

CHAPTER 3: DECEPTIONS

"Hey, guys." Jen replies.

"Hi Jen. You're so beautiful!" says Joey.

"Watch out, Joey; my friend Jen has a man." says Aileen.

"What's her man got to do with me, right Jen?" Joey jokingly responses.

"Stop playing . . . you don't even know me." says Jen defensively.

"I'm just playing, Jen. but I want to get to know you . . . if you let me." he replies.

"Let's just eat some pizza." Jen responds.

Two hours later . . .

"You are so funny, Joey. I can't believe how much we have in common . . . this has been such a fun night!" says Jen.

"It really has been! So listen, Jen. I didn't mean to disrespect you. I was really playing around earlier . . . but I am serious about how beautiful you are!" says Joey.

"Thank you, Joey. You look good too!" Jen replies.

"So, since you go to the same school as Aileen, we can pick you girls up from school and drop you off at your houses . . . if you'd like," says Joey.

"A ride home would be awesome because I hate riding the bus." Jen happily says.

"See you tomorrow, Jen!" Joeys says as he kisses her hand.

The next day at school, Jen and Aileen wait outside for their ride home.

"So, Jen, if I didn't know any better, I would think Joey kind of likes you," says Aileen.

"No! He's just a really friendly and funny guy." Jen says bashfully.

"Here comes the friendly funny guy now."

"Hey, ladies!" says Josh. We got to stop by Joey's house before we drop y'all off at home, is that ok?"

"Yeah, that's ok." Aileen responds.

When they arrive at Joey's house, Joey invites Jen to come inside for a tour and meet his parents.

"I don't know if I should." Jen reluctantly says.

"Go ahead, Jen. It won't take long; I'll wait here with Josh because we need to talk anyway." Aileen suggests.

"Ok, I'll go." says Jen.

"Ok, Jen, this is my house . . . so how do you like it?" Joey asks.

"Wow, the inside is even more beautiful!" Jen replies.

"Thanks, so we should wait a little bit because Josh and Aileen are talking about something personal outside. Come. We'll wait in my room." Joey says as he walks her over to his room.

"That's fine. By the way, where are your parents?" asks Jen.

"I guess they're not home." Joey answers.

Jen does find it suspicious that his parents aren't home. But she ignores it.

"You know, when I first met you, I thought you were a lowlife, but it turns out you're really sweet and funny. You make me feel special, and I wish my boyfriend JR would be more like you." says Jen.

"If I were your boyfriend, I would always make you feel special and wanted." Joey replies looking into her eyes.

"I think you're getting a little too close to me, Joey." she says while backing up.

"Let me make you my woman and forget about your man." Joeys says while trying to kiss her.

CHAPTER 3: DECEPTIONS

Joey continues to touch and kiss Jen. She has a battle within herself, because she knows it's wrong but is enjoying the affection she's getting.

A while later . . .

Jen and Joey walk out of the house towards the car. Jen feels awkward.

"Are you ready to go home now?" asks Aileen.
"Yeah, Aileen. I'm ready." Jen awkwardly replies.
"That was a long tour, guys," says Aileen.
"Yeah. I showed her the whole house," says Joey.

"Hey, Jen. Can I please talk to you for a second in private?" asks Joey.
"Sure you can, Joey." Jen answers.
"So, Jen, will I ever see you again?" he asks.
"Listen, Joey. I like you, but I have a boyfriend." she says.
"Are you sure you're still going to have a boyfriend after taking a tour of my house?" questions Joey.
"I don't know anymore, I feel really confused right now." Jen responds as she gets into the car.

I haven't heard from Jen in a few days; maybe she's mad at me. I should call her. Or maybe I shouldn't because I need to start keeping my distance from her. I do love her, but I'm not in love with her. I just don't want to hurt her feelings.

Work it out for me, Lord Jesus.

The next morning at school Jen looks for Aileen.

"Good morning, Aileen. Have you heard from Joey lately?" asks Jen.

"Yeah, I see him every day at Josh's house. Why do you ask, Jen?" she replies.

"Because I've been calling him every day since we went to his house, and he hasn't answered my calls." Jen says.

"Oh, Jen. I hope you're not starting to like him. He just started dating the girl that lives one house away from him. They go to the same college, and he's been trying to get with her for years." says Aileen obnoxiously.

"No way. I don't like him; I'm with JR." Jen says as tears fill her eyes.

Later that month . . .

"Jen, I haven't seen you around much lately." I say concerned about her.

"So sorry, JR. I've got too much I'm dealing with right now, JR. With all the exams coming up, prom, and graduation . . . I just don't have time to hang out." she responds.

"Are you ok, Jen? Why are you crying? Is it because of Aileen? I ask. Ever since you've started hanging out with her, you've been acting differently."

"Why are you so concerned about my friend when you've been spending a whole lot of time with Liza? Did you think I hadn't noticed? Does Tony know about it?" asks Jen with an attitude.

Whoa, Jen . . . calm down. I'm just trying to look out for you."

"Thank you, JR. There's something personal I must tell you." she says reluctantly. "Please come to my house tomorrow."

"If it's so personal, why would you tell me while your parents are home?" I ask.

"Tomorrow is Saturday, and they have some errands to run." Jen says.

"Fine, Jen. See you tomorrow."

I wonder what Jen is going to tell me. She's acting differently. I guess I'll find out tomorrow.

"Hey, Aileen. Can we leave school so we can talk? It's very serious." Jen says.

"All right, Jen. Let's go." Aileen curiously replies.

"What's going on with you, Jen?" Aileen asks.

"Ok . . . it all started a few weeks ago when Joey took me for a tour of his house. He kept trying to seduce me to sleep with him. I felt weak at that moment, and I lost my virginity to him." Jen says shamefully.

"Whoa, Jen. I just can't believe that you not only lost your virginity to Joey . . . who you only saw twice in your life, but you also cheated on JR, and you're supposed to be a church girl. And to top it all off . . . he now has a girlfriend that he loves." says Aileen.

"I know, Aileen . . . but the worst part is that I missed my period and just found out I'm pregnant." Jen says as tears stream down her face.

"Oh, my goodness, Jen! What are you going to do?" asks Aileen.

"I don't know, but what I do know is that I don't want to lose JR." she responds.

"He's probably going to leave you for this, Jen." says Aileen.

"I know, Aileen. I think he has a thing for Liza, and he might leave me for her when he finds out."

"For Liza? The girl who works at the gym and is dating Tony?" Aileen questions.

"Yeah . . . I can tell he has a thing for her." says Jen.

"I have an idea, Jen. When's the next time you see JR?" asks Aileen.

"Tomorrow morning. He wants me to tell him what's going on with me." she replies.

"Great . . . get him to sleep with you tomorrow and then wait a few weeks and tell him you're pregnant with his baby." Aileen deceitfully recommends.

"That's crazy, Aileen! He'll never fall for it because he's saving himself for marriage." Jen says.

"Listen, Jen, do you want to lose JR forever?"

"No, I don't want to lose him. I love him and want to marry him."

"So do what you got to do, Jen, and I'll work on getting Liza away from him." Aileen says.

I'm here at Jen's house waiting for the Jen to finally tell me what's bothering her.

"This is hard for me to say, JR, but I've been feeling like you kind of have a thing for Liza, and it's been making me feel like you're going to leave me to get with her." says Jen.

Oh no, she finally realized that I'm into Liza. I guess it's a good thing, but I don't want to hurt her feels.

"Where would you get an idea like that, Jen?" I nervously ask.

"Ever since your parents started hanging out together with Liza's parents, you're always with her at your house." Says Jen.

"I'm sorry you feel that way, Jen. Liza and I are just friends, that's all . . . plus, she's dating Tony." I say trying to avoid any further questions.

"Thank you for reassuring me, JR. I feel so much better now."

"Of course, Jen." I respond.

"JR, I wanna go further in our relationship."

CHAPTER 3: DECEPTIONS

"I know, Jen. We already talked about this, and I told you we'll pray about getting married."

"No, JR. I mean . . . to go all the way, and it won't be a sin because we're planning on getting married one day."

"You know we can't do that, Jen, and it is a sin . . . unless we're already married."

"Let me convince you, JR."

"Whoa, stop, Jen. I don't think you should be trying to kiss me like that." I say as I pull away from her.

"Just relax, JR, and let me do what I want to do."

"No, Jen. What's gotten into you?" I ask.

"I'm so sorry, JR. I thought that this would make me feel more secure about our relationship. Please forgive me." she says trying to make me feel sorry for her.

"Of course, I forgive you, Jen."

"JR, could you please stay and watch movies with me until my parents get home? I don't want to be here alone." she asks.

"That's fine, Jen. I'll stay, but only if you promise not to keep trying me like that."

"I won't, JR. Thank you."

Three hours later . . .

I fell asleep during the movie and suddenly I wake up with some of my clothes off.

"What happened, Jen? Why are my clothes half off?" I ask.

"What do you mean, JR . . . don't you remember?" she asks.

"Remember what? All I remember is falling asleep, Jen."

"We slept together or, should I say, we made love." she responds.

"It can't be. I would've remembered."

"Just because you don't remember doesn't mean it didn't happen." She says with a smirk on her face. "Plus, I thought you changed your mind about it because you didn't stop me, JR."

"Jen, I'm not sure what you're trying to pull here, but you know I would never consent to that. So now tell me what's going on." I sternly say.

She must think I'm dumb. I was born at night but not last night.

"Ok, JR. I'm so scared to tell you this, but I cheated on you with an older guy. He seduced me into sleeping with him, and I just found out that I'm pregnant, but I don't know what to do." she says.
"What? Where is this guy?" I ask.
"I don't know because the day after we slept together, he stopped answering my calls and is dating someone else, so he doesn't even know I'm pregnant." says Jen.
"So, were you trying to trick me into sleeping with you so you can say it's my baby?" I ask.

"Yeah, JR. I'm so sorry . . . it was Aileen's idea when I told her that I didn't want to lose you."
"That's so messed up, Jen. I can't go out with you anymore. This relationship is over."

"I know it was messed up, JR. I don't think I could've gone through with it." Jen cries as she leans on my shoulder.
"You just tried to, Jen."
"I'm so sorry, JR. Please don't break up with me. You're the best thing in my life, and I need you." she begs.

CHAPTER 3: DECEPTIONS

"I need time to think about all this, Jen; it's a lot to grasp all at once."
"Ok, JR. Take all the time you need."

"So what are you going to do now, Jen? Are you going to tell your parents?" I ask.
"I'm scared that they'll send me away for getting pregnant and on top of that, by a guy that wants nothing to do with me."
"I'll help you tell your parents, Jen. I still care about you, and I always will."
"Thank you, JR. Would you tell my parents that you're the father of the baby until I have time to figure out how to tell them what really happened?" she reluctantly asks.
"No way! I can't lie like that, Jen."
"Please, JR. I'm desperate . . . I feel like my whole world is falling apart." she pleads.
"Ok, Jen. I'll do it, but just for a little while." I reluctantly agree.
"Thank you, JR. You're the best."
"This is a lot for me to take in right now. I need to think, Jen."
"Sure, I understand." Jen says.
"I'm sorry Jen . . . I got to go."

I get home as fast as I can and run to my room. I kneel on the floor and cry out to God.

Lord, what's going on? I can't believe I agreed to do this to you, Liza, and myself. I feel bad for Jen, and I knew there was something suspect about Aileen. Jen needs me now, and I promised to be there for her, but lying to everyone is killing me. What should I do? Help me Lord, please!

It's been two weeks since I've seen Jen. It was such a shock and disappointment when she told me everything. I can't believe some college guy would take advantage of her like that. Then I agreed to lie about getting her pregnant. I'm on my way to school and I hope I see her there.

"Hey, JR. Are you ok?" asks Jen.
"Yeah, Jen. I'm sorry for running out on you the other day. I was just shocked about everything and I'm not sure if I made the right choice in saying I would help you with this." I say to her.
"Thank you for agreeing to it, JR. We do have to make it believable, so we must tell both of our parents." Jen resultantly says.
"Now you want me to lie to my parents?" I ask.
"Please, JR; just for a little while." she begs.
"Ok fine, so when are we going to tell them?" I stupidly ask.
"Alright, JR. After school, we'll go to your house and tell both of our parents then."

"I'll call my parents and let them know we need to speak with them." I say to her as I walk away.

Oh no, there's Liza. I hope she didn't hear any of that.

"Hi, Josiah!"
"Hi, Liza!"
"What's up with you, Josiah? You seem kind of distant lately. asks Liza.
"There's a lot going on right now, Liza, that I need to talk to you about another time."
"Ok, Josiah. Is it about the prom?" she asks.
"No, just something we can talk about on Friday night when you come over my house." I sadly say.
"Ok, Josiah. I'll see you at your house on Friday."
"Ok, bye, Liza!"

CHAPTER 3: DECEPTIONS

I wonder how Liza is going to react to this. She did warn me that being with Jen could ruin my chances with the woman of my dreams. After this is all over, I'm also going to tell Liza how I feel about her.

Schools out and this is the moment I've been dreading. I'm about to lie to my parents for Jen.

"Hey, JR. I hope you're ready to tell our parents." says Jen.

"Hi everyone, there's something Jen and I need to talk to you about." I say nervously.

"Ok, kids. What is it?" my parents ask.

"Well, Jen and I are having a baby." I say hesitantly.

"What?! How could you?" ask my parents while getting up from the couch.

"Yeah, how could you do this to our daughter, JR?!" say Jen's parents.

"We're so sorry; it just happened, and now we're having a baby." expresses Jen.

"Are you guys going to get married?" my mom asks.

"Well, Mom, we're still praying about getting married." I respond.

"So, you didn't need to pray before you decided to sleep together, but all of a sudden, you need to pray about marriage?" my father asks.

"You're right, Dad." I say as tears fill my eyes.

"We're all still very upset about what you kids did, but we'll take it one day at a time." Jen's dad says.

"Thanks, Dad." says Jen.

"We're going to call it a night right after we speak with Jen's parents alone." my dad says.

SECRETLY WAITING

Jen and I go to the backyard to give our parents some time alone. I feel so disgusted in lying to my parents, but I can't let Jen go through this alone.

"That went well, don't you think, JR?" asks Jen.
"No, I've never seen my parents so disappointed in me." I reply.
"Well, it would make them feel better if we would have told them we're engaged to be married." she suggested.
"I'm not going to keep lying to my parents, Jen. Don't you see that one lie leads to another?" I respond.
"I'm sorry, JR. I was kind of hoping through this, we might stay together and raise this baby as our own."
"This is too much, and I just need time to think, Jen."
"Is it that you have feelings for someone else, like Liza, maybe?" Jen questions.
"I already told you, Jen. Liza and I are friends. You're the one that cheated on me, and now you're trying to turn this around on me." I express.
"Ok, JR. I'm sorry for saying that."

Lord, I'm crying out to you. Help me! I just agreed to ruined my life. How are my parents going to trust me after this? Pease, Holy Spirit, tell me what to do!

I can't until tomorrow night. I want to sit Liza down and tell her everything.

"Liza, Liza." I shout
"What do you want, Josiah?" Liza asks while walking away from me.

"I just want to confirm for tomorrow night to hang out at my house."

Chapter 3: Deceptions

"No, Josiah. I don't think we should be friends anymore." she says.

"Why not, Liza?" I ask.

"Your parents told my parents everything that happened with you and Jen. They don't want me hanging out with a guy that got his girlfriend pregnant." she angrily responds.

"Wait, Liza; please let me explain what happened."

"I don't need to hear details about how you did it, Josiah."

"Liza, I can see you're really upset, but please let me explain." I beg.

"I am upset because now I can't trust my best friend to tell me anything." she replies.

"Are you sure you're not upset for any other reason?" I ask.

"No, I got to get home; my parents want me there right after school, so, bye, Josiah."

"Ok. Bye Liza."

Liza runs over to Tony.

"Hey, Tony, could you take me home, please?" Liza asks.

"Of course, Liza, but can I ask what's bothering you?" he asks.

"I'm fine; someone just made me a little mad." she responds.

"Ok . . . I want to ask if you'll go to the prom with me, Liza?" Tony asks.

"Yes, Tony. I'll go with you!" she says.

Lord, everything is getting worse. Liza hates me now, and so do her parents. I'm trying to help Jen, and it's costing me everything. I believe that somehow you'll work everything out for my good.

It's finally prom night and I'm here with Jen. This is not happening the way I pictured.

"Yo Liza, there's Jen and JR. Let's go sit with them." Tony suggests.

"I'd rather not, Tony. Can we spend some time alone because we're always hanging out with people?" Liza asks him.

"Ok sure, so what do you want to do?" he questions.

"Let's leave and go somewhere else." she suggests.

"Sounds good to me!"

Oh no, Liza is leaving the prom early with Tony. I hope she doesn't do anything she'll regret.

"Hi, Jen!" exclaims Aileen.

"Hey girl." Jen says as she's looking over at Liza.

"What are you looking at Jen?" asks Aileen.

"At Liza leaving with Tony, says Jen."

"Oh. It looks like they're going somewhere private," says Aileen while winking at her.

"Yes, it does," says Jen.

Prom is over and I can't stop thinking about Liza. I want to protect her from making any life changing mistakes. I hope I see her at school on Monday.

"Good morning, Liza." says Aileen while smirking.

"Good morning, Aileen. Why is everyone staring at me?" Liza asks

"Oh, it's because everyone knows that you had a really fun prom night with Tony." Aileen replies.

"What do you mean?" Lisa questions.

"Everyone knows you gave it up to Tony." Aileen says accusing Liza.

"But I didn't sleep with Tony." Liza responds.

"You can be honest, Liza; it's ok that you're that type of girl." Aileen mocks.

"But I'm not that type of girl, Aileen, so get outta my face." she says while running away in tears towards Tony.

Chapter 3: Deceptions

"Hey, Tony, did you tell people that you slept with me?" Liza asks.

"Never, but for some reason people think that we slept together, and when I tell them it didn't happen, they say that I'm trying to keep it on the low." Tony says.

"Who would spread such lie about us?" Liza asks.

"I don't know Liza, but don't cry; it doesn't matter what they think." he says as he hugs her.

"I just feel so hurt, Tony."

"Ok, Liza. I'm not trying to leave you alone in this sensitive moment, but I got to get to class." Tony says.

"It's ok, Tony. Go." Liza replies.

Wow, I just got a text from Liza! She wants me to meet her by our favorite tree after school. I let her know that I'll be there.

After school . . .

"Is everything ok, Liza?" I ask.

"No, people are spreading rumors that Tony and I slept together on prom night. You wouldn't happen to know who's saying that, would you?" Liza asks.

"No, I haven't heard that, Liza, but did that really happen?"

"No way! I'm still a virgin, but now everyone at school thinks I'm easy." she cries.

"That's crazy. They don't think that at all. I'll try to find out what happened."

"Thank you, Josiah."

"Anything for you, Liza. By the way, does this mean we're friends again?" I ask.

"I guess it does. I miss you, Josiah!" she says as she hugs me.

"I miss you too, these few weeks of us not really talking have been torture for me, Liza; so please don't ever stop talking to me again." I say as I squeeze her tight.

"I won't, Josiah."

Lord, God, you always come through with your faithfulness! I love you, Lord, and thank you for restoring my relationship with Liza.

Chapter 4: Confrontations

Today is graduation day. I'm officially a high school graduate!
"We've finally graduated high school," I shout out.

"Amen to that, Josiah!" Liza agrees.

"What's the plan now, Liza? Are we still going to stay friends even though we're not in the same school anymore?" I ask.

"Actually, Josiah, I've been praying about it, and I decided to go to community college after all." she says.

"That's great, we can be in the same school again!" I say as I hug her.

"Things are going to be a little different; you're going to be a dad in the middle of the school year," Liza says.

"There's more to that story that I still haven't told you, but for now I got to remember that God will always work out all things together for good because I love him." I respond.

"I know you'll tell me one day, when you're ready. But I do love that you always believe in God's promises!"

"Thanks, Liza. That means a lot! There's Jen. I got to go." I say while walking away.

"Bye, Josiah!"

"Congratulations, JR!" Jen exclaims.
"Same to you, Jen!" I reply.

"So, JR, now that we've both graduated and are now having a baby, have you decided if you want to raise this baby as our own?" asks Jen.

"I don't know Jen; I can't just pretend that all this isn't a lie. This isn't a good time for us to talk about this. We aren't together anymore." I sternly say.

"I'm sorry, JR. I just thought that we were past this by now and that you forgave me." Jen says.

"I did forgive you, Jen, but that doesn't mean that everything will go back to the way it was before." I express to her.

"What do you mean by that, JR? We're adults now and need to make decisions about our future."

"I need some more time to think; please understand, Jen." I sincerely say.

"Fine, JR. I got a phone call, excuse me."

Jen walks over to the side to answer a call. She must be crazy to think I will up this lie forever. I care about her, but I need to end this soon.

"Hello?"
"Is this Jen?"
"Yeah, who's this?"
"This is Joey; please don't hang up on me."
"Ok, what do you want?"

"I just wanted to say I'm sorry for what I did to you, and I hope you can forgive me." asks Joey.

"You hurt me so badly, Joey," she says with tears running down her face.

"That's why I'm calling, Jen. Can I come see you because we need to talk?" he asks.

"When?"

"I can come by and pick you up right now."

"I can't right now, but you can meet me at the pizza shop in one hour."

"Ok, Jen. See you there."

Later at the pizza shop, Jen walks in and sees Joey.
"Wow, Jen. You're still so beautiful!" Joey says.
"Thanks, Joey." she replies.
"So, Jen, ever since the day I met you, I haven't been able to stop thinking about you. Aileen told me to stop trying to get with you because you have a man and you were getting married to him. She also said that nothing would change your mind. So I tried moving on with a girl that lives on my block. I was ok for a little while because I kept reminding myself that you didn't want me. After a while, I couldn't handle it anymore because you're all I thought about, and I'm willing to fight for you. So I asked Aileen for your new number because the old one was disconnected, but she refused to give me your number until I told her how I feel about you." Joey says.

"Wow, Joey. I don't know what to say, and I can't believe that Aileen told you that." Jen says shocked at what he said.
"Jen, please tell me if I have a chance with you?" asks Joey.
"I don't know." she responds.
"Aileen told me everything." Joey says.
"Oh, she did?" asks Jen.
"Yeah, and I feel like you should think about us being a family, Jen."
"I will Joey, but I need some time to really think about it."
"Thanks, Jen. I'm going to be gone for training for my new job for four months; please keep in touch with me and let me know what you decide." Joey says.
"Ok, Joey. I will."

Jen is texting me so late. I hope everything is ok.

"Hi, JR. I'm texting you to let you know that I will tell our parents the truth about what happened in four months." Jen texts.
"Why so long, Jen?"
"That would give me enough time to work everything out, JR."
"I'll try Jen, but no more than that because this is getting out of hand."
"Ok, thank you, JR, for doing this and not telling anyone else about it."
"No problem, Jen."

Lord, why am I doing this crazy thing? Help me get out of this bind without Jen getting hurt and most of all that everyone I lied to would forgive me.

Four months later, the end of September . . .

"Hi, Tony!" Aileen says.
"Hey, Aileen!"
"Are you going to be starting at tonight's college game?" she asks.
"You know it, Aileen. Why, are you coming to the game?" asks Tony.
"Yeah, I am."
"Cool, I'll see you there later, Aileen."
"Ok, I'll be cheering for Tony!"
"Thanks!"

Later that night at the game…

"Wow, Tony, you were on fire tonight!" exclaims Aileen.
"Thanks, Aileen. You were my biggest fan tonight." Tony replies.

Chapter 4: Confrontations

"For sure, Tony. Would it be ok if you could give me a ride home? asks Aileen. My boyfriend and I broke up, so I no longer have transportation."

"Yeah, hop in." he says.

"Thanks, Tony . . . by the way, you're so hot! Aileen flirtatiously says.

"I know, you're hot too, Aileen. I don't know what kind of an idiot would break up with you."

"Thanks, Tony, but be careful. I wouldn't want Liza to get jealous."

"Don't worry about her, Aileen . . . what she doesn't know won't hurt her."

"Ok, Tony, if that's the case, why don't you come over to my house for a game night celebration?" Aileen suggests.

"Let's go!"

Four months later...

"It's great to be back home after four months of boot camp training for work!" Joey expresses.

"It's great to have you back, Joey." Jen says.

"So, Jen, now that I'm back, and you're almost six months pregnant with my baby, I've been doing a lot of thinking."

"Me too, Joey."

"Jen, will you marry me?" Joey asks while down on one knee.

"Yes, Joey. I will marry you, and I want us to be a family." she says.

"You just made me the happiest man ever, Jen. I love you, and these past four months of getting to know you have been amazing, even though it was over the phone!"

"I love you too, Joey!"

"Hello?"

"Hi, JR. It's Jen."
"What's up, Jen?"

"I wanted to let you know that you don't have to pretend anymore. I wanna tell our parents the truth tonight."

"Wow, Jen. Ok, let's do it, and may I ask why the sudden decision to do it tonight?" I ask.

"Well, JR . . . I know that you've only stayed with me these few months because you're an amazing man of God that has a loving and caring heart, and I know that you've been wanting to tell your parents the truth." she says.

"Thank you, Jen. You know that I'll still be here for you as a friend, and it feels good to finally let our parents know the truth."

"For me too, JR. I also wanted to let you know that the guy that got me pregnant contacted me, and he apologized for everything. He wants us to be a family."

"You sound happy, Jen, but what if he abandons you again?" I ask.

"He won't, JR. He said it was Aileen that told him to leave me alone, and he tried to move on, but he couldn't."

"I knew there was something shady about that girl."

"Well, I'm not trying to defend her, JR, but at the time, she didn't know what happened between the guy and me." Jen explains.

"She still told you to trick me into being your baby daddy; that speaks for itself." I remind her.

"You're right, JR. She's probably not a good person to take advice from and certainly not a good friend."

"Enough about her, tell me about this guy . . . what's his name?" I ask.

"His name is Joey." she says with a giggle.

CHAPTER 4: CONFRONTATIONS

"So did you ask Joey about how he's planning on taking care of you and the baby?"

"Yeah, we've been talking every day for the past four months. We've been getting to know each other, and we're in love." She expresses.

"Wow, Jen. I'm actually really happy for you guys! But on another note, at what time are we meeting up with our parents tonight?" I ask.

"At 6 p.m., and would you mind if Joey comes too, so he can meet them and let them know what really happened?" Jen asks.

"That would be great because I would like to know why a guy in college pressured a girl in high school to sleep with him, got her pregnant, and then abandoned her."

"Please, JR, don't act like that; you don't know the whole story." she begs.

"You're right, Jen. I'm sorry."

"See you tonight, JR."

"Alright, bye, Jen."

I'm so excited I can't stand it right! I'm finally going to be free from this trap. I gotta go tell Liza! Hallelujah! I'm heading over to Liza's house right now. I'm going to knock on her door and tell her everything.

"Who is it?" Liza asks.

"It's Josiah."

"Hi, Josiah. What are you doing here" You know my parents don't want us to hanging out." Liza expresses sternly.

"Liza, can I talk to you outside?" I ask.

"Yeah, quickly before my parents flip out." she hurries out.

"I just wanted to tell you that it's over between Jen and me."

"What? Why?"

"It's a long story, but the baby she's having isn't mine."

45

"Oh my goodness. I'm sorry that happened to you, Josiah."

"Don't be. I knew it wasn't my baby because we never slept together." I explain.

"What? You lied to me?" she asks.

"No, Liza. I told you to let me explain, but you didn't want to hear it. Then I told you that I would explain it one day"

"Don't even go there, Josiah. We started talking again . . . which means you could've told me whenever." Liza says.

"Liza, I'm sorry. I agreed to say it was my baby so Jen's life wouldn't be ruined."

"I understand you tried to do a noble thing, Josiah, but you lied to everyone you love, and you betrayed our friendship for Jen, the one you'll do anything for."

"It's not like that at all, Liza. Please forgive me."

"I do forgive you, Josiah, but I really can't do this anymore."

"I thought you would be happy when I told you this."

"Why did you think I would be happy about you breaking up with Jen?" she asks.

"Well, I thought that maybe you and I could be together Liza because you're the most fun, amazing, beautiful, and coolest person I've ever met, and I'm falling for you and thought you liked me too."

"I'm with Tony, and I'm faithful to him." she says.

"So, you don't have any feelings for me at all?" I ask.

"I do, Josiah . . . only as friends."

"Wow, Liza. I'm sorry again, and I'll be leaving now."

"Bye, Josiah, and please don't come by here again."

Lord, my God, please forgive me for all I've done against your Word. I didn't even consider how you felt about everything I agreed to. I'm sorry I ruined everything between Liza and me after you trusted me with a divine secret knowledge. You shared my deepest desire with me by showing me who would be my wife and I messed up. I'm sorry, Lord.

Later at my house, I must face my parents with this confession.

"Mom, Dad, we have something to tell you, and before we do, I just want you all to know that JR had nothing to do with this. I convinced him to agree with what I said, and he only agreed to protect me." Jen says.

"What is it, Jen?" her dad asks.
"JR and I never slept together, and the baby I'm carrying belongs to a guy named Joey." She explains.
"How did this happen, Jen? You lied to us and cheated on JR?" Jen's dad asks.
"Yes, but it wasn't planned, and we're so sorry that we lied to you all." she expresses.
"Who is this guy, and where is he?" her dad asks.
"He wants to come over to talk to you, and he wants to take responsibility for the baby and me. Jen says.
"All right, Jen. He can come over, and we'll all talk to resolve this together." Her dad says.
"Thank you all for being so understanding, I'm going to call him and let him know that he can come over now."
"My parents and I will be leaving so that you guys can all talk as a family." I say as my parents, and I start walking out.
"Ok, bye JR, bye Sofia, bye Jose." Says Jen

"Josiah, we're still shocked about this whole thing. Are you hurt by what Jen has done to you and how she convinced you to lie to us?" my parents ask.

"I guess I felt a little betrayed at first, but I also felt it was a way out." I respond.

"What do you mean by 'a way out,' Josiah?" asks my dad.

"Well, Dad, I've wanted to break up with her for a while now, but I didn't want to hurt her feelings because I still care about her and what happens to her." I explain.

"We had no idea you felt that way, but may we ask why the sudden change?" my dad asks.

"Well, I'm also really falling for someone else."

"Wait a minute, Josiah. Is it Liza?" my mom asks..

"Yes, Mom. It's Liza."

"I should've known because of the way you both are with each other. It was kind of obvious." she says.

"But she hates me now because I lied to her, and she said she wants to be with Tony, her boyfriend." I sadly say.

"Whoa, Josiah. We're sorry to hear that, but you did bring that upon yourself." my mom says.

"I know, Mom. I know."

Two months later . . .

One day until my nineteenth birthday, and I have no girlfriend or best friend. Jen married Joey a month ago, and they're having a baby in a little over a month from now. I'm happy that they're a family now. Liza and Tony are still together, and he asked her to marry him, and she said yes. She is supposed to be my wife, not Tony's, but I ruined everything because I wasn't patient enough to wait for her. I'm just going to focus on getting closer to God and paying attention in school.

I'm here at the mall today, trying to find an outfit for my birthday. I hear someone ask me a question. As I turn around, I see who it is.

Chapter 4: Confrontations

"This is the first time I've ever seen you at the mall." says Aileen

"Yeah, I'm here to buy myself something for my birthday." I reply

"Oh ok. Do you want some company, JR?" she asks.

"No thanks, Aileen. I'm good."

"Look, JR. I know you don't like me because Jen told me, but please give me a chance. I've made lots of messed up choices in life, but I'm trying to change."

"Wow, Aileen. That's very honest of you."

"Thanks, so can I shop with you?" she asks.

"Sure, why not?"

Two hours later . . .

"Well, Aileen, I had fun shopping with you, but I got to go now."

"Ok, JR. Would it be ok if you drove me home because I don't have a ride?" asks Aileen.

"All right, let's go."

"So, JR, I heard you're still a virgin; is that true?"

"Yeah, I am, Aileen, and I will stay that way until I'm married."

"What, why?" Aileen asks.

"Because I only want to be with one woman, the one God has for me."

"Well, in my opinion, JR, I think you should sleep with more than one woman so you can practice and be the best for that woman." she suggests.

"I appreciate your opinion, Aileen, but I don't think so. I wouldn't want the woman that God has for me to practice with another man, so I wouldn't do that to her. Besides, I can practice with her for her." I explain.

"I can respect that, JR; I was just hoping you could have practiced with me." she says while getting closer to me.

"Thank you, Aileen, but again, I'm saving myself."

"No problem. I was just trying to give you a hint."

"Look, Aileen, you're a very pretty girl, but you need to start respecting yourself and realize that you're special. You should be treated with respect by a man that loves you enough to wait and marry you." I encourage.

"Wow, JR. That was deep. Nobody's ever spoken to me like that before, thank you!"

"You're welcome, and listen, Aileen, I'm sorry, but I can't bring you home. I just remembered I'm going somewhere the opposite way of your house, so can you call someone else to pick you up?" I ask.

"It's ok, JR. I think I saw one of my friends here. I'll ask if I can get a ride. See you around." She says while getting out of my car.

"Ok, bye, Aileen."

Aw man, I forgot my bag at the last store I was in. I got to check if

it's still there. As I walk back into the mall. I see Tony holding hands with Aileen. I'm going to wait to see what they're doing. Oh my gosh, Aileen and Tony are all over each other. He's playing Liza. Wait, I wonder if Liza and Tony broke up? I can't even call her because she told me not to speak to her. I'll pass by her class tomorrow and try to get her to talk to me.

At school . . .

"Excuse me, Liza." I say while tapping her on the shoulder.

"What, Josiah?" Liza asks.

"I know you don't want to talk to me, but I miss you and want to know how you're doing." I sincerely say.

"I'm fine."

"How's Tony?" I ask curiously.

"He's fine. Why do you ask?"

Chapter 4: Confrontations

"I heard you guys are getting married."

"Yes, we are getting married in the summer." she says.

"Liza, please don't marry Tony; he's playing you with Aileen. I saw them all over each other at the mall last night." I explain.

"You are something else, Josiah, Tony loves me, and he wouldn't hurt or lie to me like some other people I know."

"I'm telling you the truth, Liza. I saw it myself."

"Like you told me the truth about you and Jen?" she asks.

"Fine, Liza. You don't have to believe me, but you should check for yourself. Bye and have a nice life." I say as I start walking away.

I'm tired of trying with Liza; she's always angry with me. I'm just going to forget about her for good and really move on.

Lord, I think I might have made a mistake about Liza being the one.

Five months later…

It's been five months since I've spoken to Liza. I think I'm going to be ok without her. I'm at the mall right now and I see some people I know. There's Jen with her baby and Liza's cousin Jael.

"Hi, JR!" says Jael.

"Hi, Jael. HI, Jen. How's little Joey Jr doing?" I ask Jen..

"He's four months now, and he's so smart. How 'bout you, JR?" asks Jen.

"Well, now that schools out, I'm going on a mission trip to Dominican Republic with the young adult group at church."

"Wow, that sounds great!" says Jen.

"What are you girls doing here?" I ask.

"We came to buy our dresses for Liza's wedding," says Jael.
"Oh ok."
"Aren't you going to the wedding JR?" asks Jen.
"No, I wasn't invited."
"What, why?" questions Jen.

"It's a long story, Jen."
"Well, we'd like to hear it really quickly because here comes Tony and Liza now," says Jen.
"I think I'll be leaving now. Bye Jen, bye Jael." I say as I start walking away.

"HEY, JR. WHERE ARE YOU GOING? I GOT TO TALK TO YOU," shouts Tony.
"Listen, Tony, there's nothing for us to talk about." I express.
"Yes, there is since you told my fiancée that I was playing her," says Tony while grabbing me by my shirt.
"Get off me, Tony." I say while taking his hands off my shirt.
"No, I'm going to bust you up, JR." he says.
"Alright, you want a fight? You got one, I say while putting up my fists.
"NO . . . TONY, LEAVE HIM ALONE!" screams Liza.
"Get away from me, Liza," says Tony.
I can't believe her just hit Liza. He's dead.
"DON'T TOUCH HER, TONY!" I shout.
"STOP THE FIGHT NOW, OR I'M CALLING THE COPS!" screams Jael.
"Break it up now. Everyone, get outta here before you all get arrested," says the security guard.

Later that night . . .

I need you, Lord . . . everything with Liza has been getting worse; she stopped going to church. She's going to marry Tony, who's playing her, and he even hit her when she tried to stop the fight between Tony and me. Lord, help Liza see the truth and turn her heart back to you.

Chapter 5: Mission Trip

Mission Trip . . .

I decide to go on a mission trip to Dominican Republic, where my parents were born and raised. I need this time away from all the drama and focus on God's mission for my life.

"Hola, Josiah!" says Manuel aka Manny, the guy in charge of the mission project.
"Hola, Manny!" I say, excited to be here.
"We missed you, Josiah!" says Manny.
"I missed you guys too, and I missed being here. Dominican Republic is so beautiful, I haven't been here since I was a kid, and it's still the same." I say admiring the place.
"Not exactly the same; there was a revival that took place here. The people here are on fire for the Lord." Manny expresses.
"What do you mean by that, Manny?" I ask.
"I mean people are getting healed from sicknesses, demons being cast out of people, and people delivered from things holding them back from truly serving God. It's amazing to see the people so passionate about God!" Manny excitedly says.
"I got to see this for myself, Manny!"
"Come, Josiah, I take you around."
"Wow, Manny, it's all true! The kids, families, and neighbors all caring for one another and helping those in need with love and purity! I've never seen anything like this before; this is what I want in my life." I express to him,

"You can, Josiah, by making Christ Jesus your priority and loving people the way he says to love them." Manny passionately says.

"I will Manny. I choose to." I promise to him.

My God, I'm crying out because I'm in need of your mercy. Forgive me, Lord, and help me love your people. I want more passion for you in my life, and I want to walk in the power of the Holy Spirit! Thank you, Lord, for bringing me here because I came here to bring these people knowledge of you, but they've enlightened me of your love, compassion, and power.

Three months later . . . August

It's the first back at school and I'm so excited to share the love of Christ with everyone. I've decided to make some new friends and reach out to some old ones.

"Hi, my name is Rubin, and this is my sister, Raquel. What's your name?" asks Rubin, a guy randomly standing in the hallway.

"I'm Josiah, but some people call me JR." I answer.

"We're new to this school and just trying to make some friends." says Rubin.

"Well, I can show you around and introduce you to a few people." I suggest.

"Thanks, bro. We appreciate it!"

"No problem, man."

We're walking around the school and this new girl Raquel keeps walking really close to me.

"So, JR, do you have a girlfriend?" asks Raquel.

"No, I don't, Raquel. I'm not trying to date anyone right now." I let her know nicely.

"Oh ok, so would you like to go out for dinner tonight?" she asks.

"Listen, Raquel, you seem very nice, but I told you I'm not trying to date anyone right now." I sternly say.

"No, JR, I meant as friends because I totally respect that you're not trying to date right now."

"Oh, sorry, Raquel. I feel so embarrassed. Of course, we can go out for dinner."

"It's ok. Here's my number and address . . . can you pick me up around 7:30 p.m. tonight?" she asks.

"Sure."

Even though she said this dinner is not a date, it sure feels like one.

"Hi, Raquel . . . you look amazing!" I say while admiring her outfit.

"You do too, JR." says Raquel.

"Thanks . . . by the way, I hope you like Japanese because we're going to this really good spot." I let her know.

"Yeah . . . I love Japanese food!"

"All right, then . . . let's go."

At the dinner, Raquel keeps trying to make conversation about dating.

"So, JR, why is it that such a fine guy like you doesn't have a girlfriend or chooses not to have one?" asks Raquel.

"Well . . . it's a long story, and I'll tell you one day. But just to make a long story short . . . I'm in love with the woman of my dreams, but I messed everything up." I say while gazing at the wall.

"Oh, sorry to hear that, JR."

"It's ok, Raquel. I'll eventually get over it. Let's get going; my parents texted that they need me home for something important."

"Ok."

I wonder what's the important news my parents want to tell me.

"Hey, Mom, hey Dad . . . what's up?" I ask.

"Well, Josiah, there's no easy way to say this, but your mom and I are getting a divorce," says dad.

"What?!" I ask in shock.

"We agreed to stay friends, but it's not working out." mom says.

"How can that be if you both have been married for over thirty years and have always been so in love?" I question.

"The truth is, Josiah, we've been fighting a lot lately, and we can't take it anymore," says mom as tears run down her face.

"Can't you just separate for right now and then decide if you still want to get divorced?" I argue.

"Well, we don't see the point in that, Josiah, so just be mature about this and let it be." dad says.

"I will, Dad, but you and Mom always taught me to trust in the Lord for everything, but you guys are not practicing what you preach." I say with a shacky voice while walking away.

"Josiah, wait . . ." says dad.

"No! I just need some time to think about this. I'll see you later." I say storming out of the room to cry out to God.

Oh, Lord, please intervene in my parents' lives and help them see that they're not trusting in you to fix their issues. I believe you will help them, Lord, and I believe you'll help me fix what I have messed up with my future wife. You showed me many extraordinary things on the mission trip to DR, and I'm trusting that I'm going to continue experiencing your power in my life.

At the store…

"Hey, you're back from your mission trip . . . how was it?" Jen asks.

"It was the best experience I've ever had in my life!" I let her know.

"Wow, that's great!" she exclaims.

"Thanks, Jen. So, how's the baby?" I ask.

"Little Joey Jr. is doing great; he's getting big and is a little over seven months old now."

"Wow, that's great Jen!"

"So, are you and Liza friends again?" asks Jen.

"No, I haven't seen her since the fight at the mall; besides, she's married to Tony now, and he doesn't want me around them since I ratted him out to Liza."

"Actually, JR, they postponed the wedding to December since the fight when he hit Liza for trying to stop the fight." Jen says.

"As much as I don't like Tony, he wasn't trying to hit her; he was swinging at me." I express.

"Well, the biggest reason is that a week before the wedding, a woman stopped at the gym where Liza works and told her she's Tony's wife." She explains.

"What! That's insane. When did he even get married?" I ask with my jaw dropping expression.

"I don't know, but when Liza checked it out, she found out it was true. A woman from Brazil paid Tony to married her, so she could get a green card. She told him she filed for divorce, but it was never finalized. So, they must wait until the divorce is finalized, which will be in December." she explains.

"That's crazy, Jen . . . but listen, I got to go; talk to you later."
"Ok, bye, JR."

Yes . . . thank you, Lord, for making a way for Liza and me to be together!

I race over to the gym as fast as I can, with hope of seeing Liza.

"Excuse me, is Liza here?" I ask one of the employees.
"Yes, she's in the break room. I'll get her for you." he says.
"Hey, Liza!" I exclaim.
"Hey, Josiah. What are you doing here?" Liza asks.
"I just want to talk to you really quick." I ask.
"Ok . . . go ahead."
"I just wanted to apologize for what happened at the mall with Tony." I apologize.
"It's ok, Josiah."
"I really miss my best friend, and I don't want anything to come between us ever again. Can you give me another chance?" I beg.
"I really miss you too, Josiah, but I'm engaged to Tony, and he doesn't want me to be friends with you anymore, and I have to respect that." she explains.
"I understand, Liza . . . I just really needed someone to talk about what's happening with my parents." I sadly say.
"Oh yeah, I heard, and I'm so sorry Josiah . . . I've been praying for them." Liza empathizes.
"Thank you, Liza, and I hope everything works out for you."

Whoa, I really thought that Liza and I could become close again. I'll just have to move on and make a new best friend.

CHAPTER 5: MISSION TRIP

Lord, I depend on you to help me fix this mess I've made.

Three and a half months later . . .

I get a random phone call from Raquel inviting me to get a bite to eat. I am kind of hungry, so I agreed to go with her.

"Thanks for meeting up with me, JR; I've been craving Chinese food all week." says Raquel, while savoring her chicken wings.
"Anytime, Raquel. I'll consider this my birthday dinner." I say to her.
"What, is today your birthday?" she asks.
"No, my birthday's tomorrow." I answer.
"Well . . . since tomorrow is your birthday, I'll sing you Happy Birthday tomorrow at school so everyone can know."
"Please don't embarrass me, Raquel."
"I'm gonna to have to, JR. I'm your friend."
"You know, Raquel . . . I like hanging out with you because you remind me of someone I was best friends with and who was very special to me." I say to her.
"Thanks for the compliment . . . so what happened with your best friend, JR?" she asks.
"To make a long story short, she's not allowed to be friends with me anymore because I told her that her fiancé was playing her, and he banned her from talking to me." I emotionally say.

"Do you miss her?" she asks.
"Every day."
"It sounds like she means more to you than what you're telling me." Raquel figured.
"She does, but it doesn't matter anymore . . . so let's get back to talking about something else." I say, trying to change the subject.

"Ok, if you insist."

I look over at the door of the restaurant; my heart begins beating so fast, and I feel like I can't even breathe.

"Hi, Josiah." says Liza with a big smile.
"Hey, Liza. What are you doing here?" I ask, mesmerized by her beauty.
"Tony and I were hungry, so I came here to get our take-out order." she says.
"Oh ok. It's good to see you again, Liza." I say trying to avoid eye contact.
"Who's your friend, Josiah?" asks Liza.
"Oh, this is Raquel, a friend from school." I respond.
"It's nice to meet you, Raquel." Liza says.
"Nice to meet you too!" says Raquel.

"My food is ready. I hope you guys have a fun date," says Liza as she walks away.
"This is not a date, Liza; she's just my friend," I nervously answer.

Wow, she takes my breath away every time I see her. I keep saying that I'm going to forget about her, but I can't.

"Wow, JR . . . was that her?" Raquel asks.
"Yeah, that's her. How'd you guess?" I ask.
"I knew by the way you looked at her and how nervous you sounded talking to her." Raquel says, while smiling.
"Yeah . . . I try not to show it."
"Try harder next time!" she says.
"I will, but it's getting kind of late, and I got to go, Raquel."
"Ok, bye"

Chapter 5: Mission Trip

I'm heading home and I still feel hurt about my parents filing for divorce. I just take it day by day.

"Hi, Mom. How yah doing today?" I ask.

"Hi, Josiah. I'm doing great since your father, and I decided to go to counseling at church." mom says.

"Really, Mom?" I ask.

"Yeah, we've been trying to work out our issues. We even had dinner tonight, and it felt like the spark is back. I thank God for this." Mom says like if she's floating on air.

"Wow, Mom. I'm so excited for you guys, and I pray that God restores your beautiful marriage." I encourage.

"Thank you, Josiah, and tomorrow night, we're going to take you out for dinner to celebrate your twentieth birthday!" she says.

"Thanks, Mom. I'd be honored."

As I start walking towards my room, I hear the doorbell ring. I answer the door and I got the biggest shock of my life.

"Liza?" I ask with my mouth wide open in shock.

"Hi, Josiah. I'm so sorry to bother you like this, but can I come in?" asks Liza as tears stream down her face.

"Yeah, sure. Is everything ok? You look like you were in a fight."

"I was in a fight, and I'm not ok, Josiah." she cries.

"What . . . why . . . with who?" I ask with concern.

"When I got to Tony's house with the food, he was in the car with Aileen, and they were making out . . . so I grabbed her by the hair and pulled her out of the window, and we started fighting," cries Liza.

"Whoa, that's crazy, Liza."

The worst part was that Tony picked her up and told me to leave her alone. So, I took the food and threw it at them both . . . and I came over here to see you." she says.

   "Are you going to be ok?" I ask.
   "Yeah, it's over between Tony and me . . . and honestly, I'm ok with that."
   "I'm so sorry you had to go through that, Liza." I say.
   "I should've believed you, Josiah. I'm sorry."
   "It's ok, Liza. I understand why you didn't trust me then." I reassure her.
   "Can I stay here with you until I calm down? I have such a bad headache." she asks.
   "Anything for you, Liza. You can stay as long as you need to."
   "Thank you, Josiah."

The next morning . . .

   "Oh my goodness, Josiah, we must've fallen asleep." Liza says.
   "Yeah, we did. Don't worry, Liza. I didn't take advantage of you." I respond.
   "I know you didn't. By the way, happy birthday!" she says while giving me a hug.
   "Thanks, Liza! How's your head feeling?" I ask.
   "It's better now . . . but I got to go get ready for school and then go cancel everything for the wedding."
   "Look, Liza, I'm not trying to tell you what to do, but I do hope that this means we can start over and be friends again."

   "Yes, Josiah, and I don't want anything or anyone to come between us anymore." says Liza.
   "I won't let that happen, Liza." I say.
   "Ok, I got to go home to get ready for school." she says.

"Ok. By the way, would you like to have dinner with my parents and me tonight for my birthday?" I ask as Liza runs out of the house.

"I would love to, and by the way, I'm so happy to hear that your parents are getting along," says Liza as she runs into her car.

"Thanks! They're actually back together since last night."

"Awesome, Josiah. See you tonight!" Liza exclaims.

My birthday is in a few minutes and God has blessed me with the best gifts. My parents back together and Liza is my best friend again.

"We're here tonight to celebrate your very special day; happy birthday, Josiah . . . we love you!" my parents say.

"Thanks, Mom and Dad! This is truly a special birthday for me!"

"You're twenty years old now, and you're pursuing your dream of going into ministry; you're blessed," says dad.

"Thanks. I give God all the glory! I also want to thank God for you both and for Liza being back in my life." I reply.

"Thank you, Josiah. I'm glad God brought us together as best friends again." Liza says.

"Thanks for this great birthday celebration. Liza and I are going to get going now, but I hope you and Mom enjoy your date tonight." I saw while winking at my dad.

"Ok, bye Josiah and Liza!" my parents answer as they snuggle together.

"So, Liza, what do you want to do tonight?" I ask.

"I want to sit on the beach and talk." she says.

"Ok, let's do it."

We're at the beach and it's a beautiful night with the woman of my dreams.

"Josiah, I wanted to let you know that I've been falling in love with you ever since the day we saw each other in Walmart." Liza confesses.

"What? And you didn't tell me or show it?" I say a little confused.

"Well, you had a girlfriend, and I had a boyfriend." she says.

"Wow, Liza. That's crazy because I'm in love with you, and I have been since the day we met." I confess.

"So that's why you used to act so weird around me." she asks.

"Yup, that's why." I say with a giggle.

"I didn't think you liked me in that way, so I stayed dating Tony. Then I thought you were going to marry Jen and have a baby, so I tried to convince myself that Tony and I should be together." Liza says.

"That's crazy because I couldn't tell if you liked me or not, so I continued dating Jen. Then when I finally got the guts to tell you how I felt about you, everything got messed up because of what happened with Jen being pregnant." I explained.

"I guess we both messed it up, Josiah." she says giggling.

"Yeah, but God gave us a second chance, Liza."

"Yes, he did." she says while gazing into my eyes.

"Would you be my girl, Liza?" I ask.

"I thought you'd never ask, Josiah!" Liza replies with an English accent.

"Is that a yes?" I ask.

"Duh! Of course, it is!" she says.

My God, my God, you are so faithful . . . even when we've messed up. You made a way for it to still work out! Thank you, my King!

Chapter 6: Broken

One month later . . . January

Liza and I have been dating for a month. I feel like the most blessed man in the world.

"My headaches have been getting worse, Josiah." Liza comments.

"You should have a doctor check it out, Liza." I suggest.

"I already called, and I have an appointment tomorrow morning. Would you please come with me?" she asks.

"I can't, Liza; it's too much of a short notice for my job, but I'll see if I can get out early and meet you there." I let her know.

"Ok, thanks, Josiah."

At the doctor's . . .

"Good morning, Miss Elisheba Nuñez. It's nice to meet you. My name is Dr. Trent."

"Hi, Dr. Trent. You can call me Liza."

"Ok, Liza, we're going to run some tests to rule some things out." says the doctor.

"Do you think something is seriously wrong with me?" Liza nervously asks.

"There's no need to worry Liza because it might just be migraines," says Dr. Trent.

"So when will you run these tests? I'm in a lot of pain." asks Liza.

"Well . . . we do have a diagnostic center that we work with, and I can squeeze you in for tomorrow morning, but you must fast for these tests," says the doctor.

"Ok, thank you," says Liza as she walks toward the door.

"Alright, see you in the morning at 7 a.m." he says.

I speed up to Liza's doctor's office, disappointed that I didn't make it to her appointment on time.

"Hi, Liza . . . sorry I didn't make it in time. What did the doctor say?" Josiah desperately asks.

"It's ok, Josiah. He said he'll run some tests in the morning, but he

doesn't think it's anything to worry about." Liza says.

"I'm coming with you tomorrow, Liza." I let her know.

"What if you're not be able to take off?" asks Liza.

"I'll tell my manager it's an emergency, and I need to be there with you."

"Ok, thank you for being here for me," says Liza as she hugs me.

The next morning . . .

"Excuse me, how much longer will Liza Nuñez be in for testing?" I ask.

"Miss Nuñez will be out of testing in just a minute," says the medical assistant.

"What's taking so long?" I nervously ask.

"Well . . . there was a situation that needed to be checked out," the medical assistant replies."3

"What do mean by 'situation?'" I suspiciously ask.

"Are you one of her relatives?" asks the MA.

"I'm Josiah, her boyfriend." I say to her.

"I'm sorry, Josiah. I can't give you any information . . . just wait until she comes out," the MA rudely responds.

"Fine, I'll wait," I say while pacing back and forth.

Now I'm nervous because of some situation they won't tell me about.

"Mr. Josiah Fernandez?" asks Dr. Trent.

"I'M JOSIAH FERNANDEZ!" I shout.

"Ms. Nuñez said it was ok to speak with you about her," Dr. Trent says.

"Ok, I'm listening, Doc," I say to him.

"We found a tumor in her brain, which is causing her headaches. We need to do a biopsy and remove it," says Dr. Trent.

"That's crazy, Doc. I just wanna see her, please," I say as tears run down my face.

"Yes, you can see her. Come with me," Dr. Trent says as he his eyes fill with tears.

"Liza!" I cry out as I hug her.

"I'm ok, Josiah." Liza says.

"I can't believe this is happening to you, Liza."

"The Lord will get me through this, Josiah. You'll see."

"How are you so calm, Liza?" I confusedly ask.

"I'm calm because my hope is in Jesus," says Liza.

"You're right, Liza. Jesus is our hope."

"I have to go to the hospital in two days for them to remove this tumor and biopsy it, but first, they will do another scan on me before we can leave to see if the tumor has spread anywhere else." she says.

"Ok, Liza. I'm here with you, and I'm gonna call your parents to let them know." I let her know.

"Thank you, Josiah."

"Well, how'd it go, Doc?" asks Josiah.

"The tumor in her head is benign, which means it is non-cancerous, but they did find one in her breast that is malignant, which is cancerous. So we will set her up for surgery next week to remove both tumors," says Dr. Trent.

"Where is she?" I ask as tears heavily flow down my face.

"Here she comes now, Josiah." Say the doctor.

"Liza, I'm so sorry," I cry.

"I'm so overwhelmed, Josiah. I just want to go home," says Liza.

"I'll take you home. By the way, Liza, your parents didn't answer the phone."

"It's ok, Josiah; just get me out of here."

My God, help us! You are the God of miracles, and I believe in you. Heal Liza, Lord, in the name of JESUS.

I'm at work and I can't focus. I need to speak to my manager.

"Wassup, JR? How's Liza doing?" asks Ricky, my manager.

"Not good, Ricky," I say.

"Look, JR, I know this is a difficult time for you and your girlfriend, but I can't let you keep taking off of work; we need you here." He says to me.

"I must be there with Liza through this. She's going through a life or death situation!" I say raising his voice.

"I'm sorry, JR. The most I can do is let you leave earlier, but you must come in," Ricky says.

"Fine Ricky, but don't expect me to stay here any extra time," I agree.

The day of the surgery . . .

Oh my God, I'm begging you to let everything go great. I believe that you have already given Liza the victory!

I call Liza from work to let her know that I love her, and I'll be there before she gets out of surgery. I will be praying the whole time. She sounded very nervous and told me she loves me about ten times.

After the surgery . . .

"Mr. Fernandez?" Asks Dr. Trent.
"Yes, Doctor?" I ask.
"She's in recovery and almost ready for you to see her, and I have great news," says Dr. Trent.

"What's the great news, Doc?" I anxiously ask.
"When we went to remove the tumor from her brain, I noticed that the tumor was a lot smaller than last week, and the one on her breast was completely gone. It's a miracle," says Dr. Trent. "I've never seen this happen in all my twenty-four years of practice."
"That's because JESUS HEALED HER!" I shout. "THANK YOU, MY LORD JESUS!"
"I heard of God doing miracles like this in the Bible, but this is my first time seeing it; wow, I think I'm going to start praying for all my patients." Says Dr. Trent.
"You should definitely pray for them all, Doc. God is amazing!" I exclaim as I praise the Lord!
"Well, ok, you can see Liza now," says Dr. Trent.

"Hi, mama . . . how are you feeling?" I ask.
"I feel a little groggy but really good overall," slurs Liza.
"That's because God is great!" I let her know.
"Yes, He is, Josiah. The Lord healed me—before the surgery, I heard the Holy Spirit tell me to decree and declare my healing

in the name of Jesus because He promised it in His Word. So I kept repeating, 'by the stripes of Jesus, I am healed.'" Liza says.

"I love you, woman of God!" I say, and I kiss Liza on the forehead.

"I love you too, man of God!" says Liza.

"Your parents are in the waiting room, and they want to see you," I let her know.

"Please tell them to come in when you leave, Josiah."
"I will, Liza. I'll check on you tomorrow morning when go home."
"Ok, Josiah. I love you!"
"I love you too, Liza!"

One month later . . .

It's been a month since Liza's surgery and things are going great!

"Wow, these potatoes taste so good, Josiah!" Liza expresses.
"I'm so happy you like them," I brag.
"I'm blessed to be here with you tonight!" says Liza as she holds my hand.

"Liza . . . I brought you here to let you know that I love you. You're the most amazing woman I have ever met, and I want to spend the rest of my life with you . . . will you marry me?" I ask while down on one knee.

"Oh my goodness, Josiah! I love you too, and I do want to spend the rest of my life with you, but I can't marry you right now." she says.

"What? Why not, Liza?" I ask.

"I'm so sorry, Josiah; ever since this whole thing happened with me having cancer and Jesus healing me, it's made me a different person. I look at life differently now, and there's a purpose that God has for me." says Liza.

"Whatever the purpose is, we can do it together, Liza, as husband and wife," I desperately respond.

"I do want to be your wife, Josiah, but not right now" says Liza.

"Why didn't you tell me how you felt sooner?" I ask.

"I was going to tell you before, but I wanted to be sure this is what I really wanted to do . . . so I was waiting until I got accepted," Liza says.

"Accepted for what?" I ask.

"Accepted to NYU!"

"So when are you supposed to find out if you got accepted?" I ask.

"I actually got the letter this morning, and I got accepted." she says.

I can't believe she kept this from. I feel so hurt and betrayed by the woman that I love. I thought she cares about our relationship.

I need to pretend to be supportive for now, so she won't get defensive.

"So when were you planning on leaving?" I ask with a disappointed look.

"I was planning on leaving in a month," says Liza as she tries to avoid eye contact.

"Ok . . . I have to respect that. So what are you going to major in, Liza?"

"Look, Josiah, I feel in my heart that God wants me to move to New York and attend NYU so that I can become a doctor," says Liza.

That's it, now she's trying to say God told her to do this. God always sends confirmation about what He tells a person to do. She's just going by her emotions because of what she went through. She's not even thinking about us.

"Wow, Liza . . . if God told you this, then there's nothing I can do about it, but I won't wait around for you. God has things for me to do that I can't stop and wait for anyone," I say as I get up from my chair. I sternly say trying not to cry.

"Are you breaking up with me, Josiah?" she asks.

"Yeah, Liza. I wish you the best, and I hope you have a nice life."

"Fine, Josiah. I will," Liza says as she cries in her seat.

I leave the table and head to my room. I can't face her right now. I'll just stay here until she leaves my house. I'm so confused that I need to pray.

Father God, I know you have told me what you want me to do in life and since what Liza thinks she's called to do is not with me, then one of us is not hearing from you. It's either she's the one for me, but she's walking away to pursue what she wants, or she's not the one. Either way, she's out of my life.

Four and a half months later . . .

Graduation day . . . End of May

It's my graduation day and I feel excited. I haven't seen Liza since she left for New York. I'm just trying not to think about her anymore.

CHAPTER 6: BROKEN

"Congratulations on graduating college, Josiah!" my parents exclaim.

"Thank you, Mom and Dad!" I joyously exclaim.

"Aren't you glad that you did dual enrollment in high school, so you only had to do two years of college?" asks mom as she wipes her lipstick off my cheek.

"Yeah. I thank God for you both for not allowing me to slack off."

"So, Josiah, I know you're going to celebrate with your cousin Ruben and friends on this cruise vacation you all planned, but please be careful out there, and don't do anything you'll regret," says dad with a serious look on his face.

"I know, Dad. I won't do anything dumb." I reassure him.

"Remember who you represent, son." dad says.

"I will always represent Christ in the right way, Dad." I reply.

"That makes us feel better about you going on this cruise," says mom.

Chapter 7: Graduation Cruise

It's cruise time! I'm excited to get away from home with my friends and have fun.

"THIS CRUISE IS SO DOPE, JR!" shouts my cousin Ruben over the sound of the crowd of people.

"I KNOW, RUBEN; THIS IS THE BEST TRIP I HAVE EVER BEEN ON!" I shout back.

"This is amazing! Thank God we could all be on this cruise vacation together!" Jael says.

"Alright everyone, we're having dinner tonight, and we must be formally dressed," says Ruben.

"Ok, see you all in one hour," everyone agrees.

I'm getting ready for dinner, and I want to make sure that I look good. You never know who I'll meet on this cruise.

"Wow, JR, you look good in a suit!" says Jael.

"Thanks, Jael . . . you look slammin'!" I say as I admire her beauty.

"Thank you!" Jael says with smile as we walk into the dining room laughing together.

Dinner is going great, but I can't wait to explore the rest of this ship.

"Dinner was great guys, and I'm going to head to my room now. Ruben says to everyone.

"Goodnight, Ruben," everyone says.

Goodnight, everyone!" says Ruben.

"I'm going to take a tour of the ship," I say.

"I'll come with you, JR," Jael says as she grabs her purse.

"Ok, let's go, Jael."

An hour later…

"This ship is huge, JR." Jael says.

"It sure is, Jael." I reply.

"You know, JR, I've never drunk wine before, and I think I feel a little tipsy," Jael giggles.

"Same here, Jael . . . I believe drinking can make people do and say things they shouldn't." I explain.

"You're right, JR. I believe it even gives people feelings that they should never entertain," says Jael.

"Jael . . ." I say as I stare into her eyes. "Your lips look so soft."

"Really, JR?" asks Jael.

"Yeah," I say as I kiss her.

"Wow, that was an amazing kiss, JR," Jael says in shock, having realized JR has kissed her.

"Do you want to come to my room?" I ask.

"I . . . I really want to, but I don't know if I should, JR." she studders.

"It's ok, Jael. It's just to talk." I beg.

"All right, JR, but only for a few minutes."

Fifteen minutes later . . .

"It's getting late, and we're still here talking," says Jael.

Chapter 7: Graduation Cruise

"I'm really enjoying your company, Jael." I let her know.

"Can I ask you a question, JR?"

"Sure, Jael. Ask away."

"Do you still have feelings for my cousin Liza?" Jael asks.

"Honestly, Jael . . . I'm not sure. For the first month that she was gone, I thought about her every day, but since then, I haven't thought about her much. I just want to forget her," I say convincingly.

"I just wanted to know since you kissed me?" she asks.

"I didn't plan it, Jael. I know I shouldn't have done that, but I'm glad I did, though."

"Really . . . why, JR?" asks Jael.

"Yeah, Jael. You're so special, and I'm starting to have feelings for you." I say.

"I didn't think you ever noticed me because of Liza."

"I did notice you, Jael, but I thought Liza was the one for me, so I never entertained it," I explain.

"I never knew, JR."

"Let's forget about Liza and have a great time".

"Ok, JR, but I have to go back to my room before we do something we'll regret." she says.

"No . . . Jael, please stay with me tonight," I suggest.

"I can't, JR . . . I'm a virgin, and I don't want to risk losing my virginity without being married," says Jael.

"It's ok, Jael. I'm a virgin and waiting to get married too," I agree.

"This is still a tempting situation," she says.

"These past few months of hanging out with you in school have been great, and I desire you so much," he says.

"I desire you too, JR, and for that reason, I'm calling it a night," Jael says as she walks toward the door of the room.

"Goodnight, Jael," I say as I watch Jael leave the room.

That was close. Even though Jael is Liza's cousin; I can't help the feelings that I'm starting to have for her. She's not as beautiful as Liza but she is an amazing woman.

Oh Lord God, thank you for preventing us both from doing something we'd regret. Now knowing that Jael is still a virgin and how serious she is about waiting makes me desire her even more, Lord.

The next morning . . . on deck

"Good morning, everyone . . . today, I want everyone to have fun; roam the boat, and we'll meet up at 6 p.m. for dinner," says Ruben.
"Let's go to the pool." Jael suggests.
"Ok, I wanted to go swimming!" I respond.

"We got to get our bathing suits from our rooms," she says.
"Alright, JR, you wait here while I change in the bathroom."
"Ok, I sigh."
"Whoa, Jael. Your bathing suit looks so good on you!" I say as look her up and down.
"Why . . . thank you, JR. Let's get yours now."
"Wait, can I hug you for a second?" I ask.
"Ok, JR; just one hug," she responds.
"It feels so good to hold you, Jael. I want to hold you forever," I say to her.
"I feel the same way about you, JR." Jael says.
"You drive me crazy, Jael. I'm so attracted to you, and I'm in love with you!" I exclaim.
'How do you know you're in love with me?" asks Jael.
"I can't stop thinking about you. These past three months that we've been hanging around each other; I get excited just

Chapter 7: Graduation Cruise

knowing you're around. I think I want you to be my wife," I say confidently.

"What . . . really? Are you sure about this?" she asks.

"Yes, Jael. I wanna be married to you; you're so beautiful, so cool, super smart, and you love God; you're like the perfect woman," I passionately say.

"I'm shocked, JR; this feels so surreal," says Jael.

"So, Jael . . . will you marry me?" I ask.

"Yes, JR. I'll marry you!" she says as she hugs me.

"Can you spend the night with me, Jael?" I ask.

"I thought you were also saving yourself for marriage?" asks Jael.

"I am saving myself for my wife, and you're gonna be my wife. Plus, we're gonna be married right away as soon as we get back home, so it's the same thing," I suggest.

"That's true, JR," she says. "We can get married at the courthouse first, and then we'll plan a wedding with all of our family and friends."

"I'm so excited to be your husband, Jael, so spend the night with me." I beg.

"All right, JR. I'll spend the night with you on one condition." she says.

"What's that?" I ask.

"Only if no one knows about it," Jael says.

"Agreed."

"So let's go to the pool for a while, then get ready for dinner with everyone else," says Jael.

"Ok, Jael, and after dinner, go to your room, and I'll meet you there after everyone goes to bed," I instruct.

Wow, I'm excited about spending the rest of my life with Jael. I can't wait until tonight.

"I have an announcement to make," I say to everyone at our table.

"Alright, JR; what is it?" everyone asks.

"I asked Jael to marry me, and she said yes."

"Congratulations to you both!" everyone says as they all hug each other."

"Thank you, we don't want to wait around . . . we will get married at the courthouse as soon as we get back home, and then have a wedding," says Jael.

"Let's celebrate with these two lovebirds!" says Ruben.

After dinner, I say goodnight to everyone. Then Ruben comes up to me and wants to talk. I hope he makes it quick, because I can't wait to be alone with Jael.

"What's up, Ruben?" I ask.

"I just wanted to know if you and Jael have slept together?" he asks.

"No, why would you even ask something like that, Ruben?" I nervously ask.

"I just want to make sure that you guys don't do anything stupid before you get married . . . from a friend to a friend. I care about you both, man," says Ruben.

"We won't, Ruben," I stutter.

"Listen, JR, I want to be your accountability partner to help you resist temptation and make sure you honor God," says Ruben.

"Oh, ok sure . . . I would like that." I reassure him.

"Great, I'm glad you agreed. I'm going to get the rest of the guys, and we're all going to stay in the same room together so you won't be tempted," says Ruben.

"I'm really tired tonight, Ruben. I prefer to be alone," I say while yawning.

Chapter 7: Graduation Cruise

"All right, JR. I'll just guard in front of your room because tonight is the last night of the cruise, and I don't want the devil to put thoughts in your head," says Ruben.

"You don't have to do this, Ruben. You're being a little extra," I express to him.

"I'm trying to look out for you, and this is something that I need to do," says Ruben.

"Ok, fine, Ruben. Goodnight," I say with an attitude.

Ring . . . ring . . .

"Hi, Jael. I just wanted to let you know that I'm gonna have to cancel for tonight because Ruben is guarding my room. He says it's so we won't do anything stupid on our last night." I explain.

"Ha, that's what I call divine intervention, JR," laughed Jael.

"It really is. I feel bad that we were gonna to do that to the Lord."

"Me too, JR. We really have great friends." she says.

Wow Lord, You really look out for me. I'm so sorry that I was planning to sin against You. I will be patient and wait until my wedding night.

"It's time to plan our wedding, JR" says Jael.

"I know . . . I'm so excited!" I exclaim.

"When should we get married?" Jael asks.

"I can't wait for you to be my wife, so if it's ok with you, I would like us to get married next weekend at the courthouse," I say.

"I don't care about a big wedding, but I would like to have a small wedding at church with our closest family and friends," she says.

"Ok, let's talk to the pastor," I respond.

I spoke to my pastor and let him know that Jael and I want to be married. He was kind of curious about the engagement. He mentioned that he didn't feel in his spirit that Jael is the one for me. I had to explain that I believe she is. So, he agreed to do our premarital consulting and perform our ceremony.

"Hi, Pastor Hope." I say while hoping to rush this.

"Hi Josiah and Jael, let's get started on our premarital counseling. It will be for two weeks," says Pastor Hope.

"We're ready," says Jael.

"I want you both to make a list of everything you dislike about each other but don't show it to each other yet," Pastor Hope says.

"Ok, Pastor, but I must warn you, there's nothing about Jael that I dislike," I express.

"That's fine, Josiah; just sit and think about anything you would like her to improve on," pastor responds.

"Ok," I say.

"Now I want you to exchange your list with each other, and please don't get offended; it's just an exercise," says Pastor Hope.

Two minutes later . . .

"How do you feel after reading Josiah's list, Jael?" asks Pastor Hope.

"I feel like I want to improve in all these areas to be the best wife for JR," she says.

"How 'bout you, Josiah?" asks Pastor Hope.

"I'm feeling a little insecure, but I'll do whatever it takes to be an awesome husband for Jael," I say with a sad countenance.

"Great exercise, guys. See you both in two days for the next session," says Pastor Hope.

I'm happy Pastor Hope agreed to counsel us, but this exercise made me feel insecure. I almost don't want to continue this.

Chapter 7: Graduation Cruise

Two weeks later . . .

"Alright . . . this is the last session of your counseling, and I need to know if any of you have feelings for anyone else?" asks Pastor Hope.

"I don't have feelings for anyone else but JR," says Jael.

"I don't have feelings for anyone else but Jael," I say doubtfully.

"Are you sure, Josiah? I do remember that you had strong feelings for Liza and Jen not too long ago," Pastor Hope responds.

"I did at one point, but the way I feel for Jael is beyond that," I reply.

"As long as you're sure, Josiah, and based on everything we talked about in every session, I believe you two will have a blessed marriage," says Pastor Hope.

"YAY! THANK YOU, PASTOR HOPE!" I shout as I hug Jael.

"Congratulations, you guys!" says Pastor Hope.

I'm very excited that I'm going to get married, but I can't stop thinking about what Pastor Hope said. I think I still have feelings for Liza but I must suppress them so I can be happy. Although, I do wonder what she's doing and if she still thinks of me.

Chapter 8: The Wedding

One month later . . . mid-July

Tomorrow is my wedding day. I'm at the church and we're rehearsing for tomorrow. I don't know how I'm going to feel when I see Liza, since I haven't seen her in so long. I feel so confused right now. I think the devil is putting these thoughts in my head. I'm just going to think positive thoughts about Jael.

"You're a blessed man, JR!" says Ruben.
"Thanks, Ruben!"
"You know Liza is in town for the wedding," says Ruben.
"I know she has to be here for Jael, but I don't care," I say defensively.
"Sorry, bro. I just wanted to let you know," replies Ruben.
"I'm sorry for coming off like that, Ruben; it's just that I'm in love with Jael, and I don't want anything to ruin it," I express.

"I now pronounce you husband and wife . . . you may kiss the bride!" says Pastor Hope.

"This was a great wedding rehearsal!" exclaims Ruben.
"Congratulations, Josiah!" says Liza.
"Thank you, Liza," I awkwardly respond.

Wow, Liza looks even more beautiful than I remember. I must remain calm and not look at her for too long.

"I hope you guys have a great wedding tomorrow," says Liza.

"Thanks. I hope you have a blessed life, Liza," I reply.

"Thank you, Josiah. By the way, I'm really enjoying medical school." she says trying to start conversation.

"It's great to hear, Liza. I gotta go see my future wife now; see you around," I respond.

"Josiah, wait," says Liza as she grabs my hand.

"What do you want, Liza?" I ask.

"I just wanted you to know that I feel really hurt that you're now marrying my cousin . . . knowing that I still love you," she says.

"What . . . why would you tell me this now, Liza?" I ask as I put my hands over my face.

"I tried not to say anything, Josiah; I just can't live without you," she cries.

"You made your choice, Liza, when you decided to leave me to go to New York," I express.

"I will always love you, Josiah. I know you were meant for me and not Jael," Liza says as tears run down her face.

"What makes you so sure about that, Liza?" I ask.

"When I was a kid . . . I had a dream about the man I would marry, and it was you, Josiah. The day I met you, I knew it was you, but I was too scared to say anything," says Liza.

"If you knew, then why did you leave me?" I ask.

"I thought you would wait for me to pursue my medical degree, but I should have waited for God to direct me. I should've married you when you asked me," says Liza.

"I'm so confused right now, Liza. I don't know what to do," I say.

"Tell me that you don't love me anymore, and I'll leave you alone forever," says Liza.

"I'm about to marry Jael tomorrow," I explain.

Chapter 8: The Wedding

"That's true, but it's not official yet, and I know that you've always said you would only marry a woman that was saving herself for marriage, but Jael is not even a virgin," says Liza.

"So, you're lying to me now?" I ask.

"No, it's true; she slept with a guy she met in college. All you need to do is ask her." Liza says.

"I will ask her."

"I wouldn't lie to you, Josiah; I love you with all my heart," says Liza.

"I do love you Liza, but I'm trying so hard not to," I say.

"Then don't marry her, Josiah." She urges.

"I can't do that, Liza. I got to go," I say as I walk away.

I'm still in shock about Liza's feelings for me. Seeing her today made me realize that I'm still crazy about her. I also can't believe that Jael wouldn't tell me about her not being a virgin. She said she was waiting for marriage. I'm going to talk to her and get the truth.

"Jael . . . I need to speak with you," I say.

"Ok, JR. What's up? You look a little outta breath," Jael says.

"Did you lie to me about being a virgin?" I ask.

"Why would you ask me that, JR?" she asks.

"Just answer me, Jael."

"No, JR. I'm not a virgin. I slept with a guy at school," she cries.

"Why didn't you tell me? Why did you lie about it?" I ask.

"I didn't tell you because everyone knows you wanted your future wife to be a virgin," she replies.

"I would've looked past it because I really wanted to be with you," I explain.

"I should've told you the truth, JR. I'm sorry," says Jael.

"So when did this happen?" JR asks.

"It happened eight months ago at a frat party." she says.

"What . . . that wasn't long ago, and you were going to sleep with me?" I ask with disgust.

"You wanted to sleep with me too, JR," she says.

"Well, what happened with that guy?" I ask.

"We slept together several times, and I thought we would be together, but he left me for his ex-girlfriend." she says with a shaky voice.

"If he didn't leave you, would you have married me?" I ask.

"Probably not. I was really in love with him," she replies.

"Do you still love him?"

"Not anymore, I think," she says.

"Wow, I can't believe this is happening right now," I say.

"JR, may I ask how you found out about this?" she asks.

"Liza told me about it."

"Oh no she didn't; she needs to butt outta my life. But let me guess, you still have feelings for her, don't you, JR?" Jael asks while looking me in the eyes.

"Of course, I still love her. I was trying to suppress my feelings because she left me to pursue school in New York." I explain.

"How could you say that JR, if you're about to marry me?" asks Jael."

"I said it because I love you too, Jael. You're great, and I was hoping we could be happy together, but you're a liar," I express.

"How dare you say that to me?" she asks.

"I can't be your husband, Jael," I tell her.

"YOU'RE THE LIAR, she says I CAN'T BELIEVE YOU WERE GOING TO MARRY ME KNOWING THAT YOU STILL LOVE HER," Jael screams.

"This is what happens when I try to settle for second best," I say as I leave the room.

Chapter 8: The Wedding

"I hate you, JR," shouts Jael. *Lord, what have I done again? I don't know what to do. I love Jael, but I'm not in love with her. I have a feeling deep within that she's not the one you have for me. I believe that Liza is the one You showed me would be my wife. She even had a dream as a kid that I was the one for her, just like You did for me as a kid. I was trying to deny it because she hurt me so bad by leaving. Guide me, Lord.*

Four months later . . .

Pastor Hope has been working with me for the past four months.

He really helped me remember that the Lord is the most important person in my life, and I need to let him guide my decisions.

"You've come a long way since all that craziness you went through," says Pastor Hope.

"You're right, Pastor. I thought I would never get back on track," I say.

"Thank God for delivering you from marrying the wrong woman and keeping you from heartache," says Pastor Hope.

"Yeah, Pastor. You're right," I say thinking about it.

"Next week is Thanksgiving, and I will be out of town, so we will have a mentoring session the week after," says Pastor Hope.

"Ok, Pastor. Have fun on your vacation."

"Thank you, and I hope you have fun with your family and friends, even though you might see Liza again," replies Pastor Hope.

"I hope I don't see her, Pastor . . . even though we agreed to be friends again, but I just don't want any drama from the past," I explain.

"Ok, Josiah. I'll be praying for God's will to be done in your life," pastor says.

Thanksgiving is at Liza's parents' house this year. I think I can handle it because, Pastor Hope has helped me.

"Welcome, everyone. It's great to have you all together again in thanking our Lord God for all his goodness!" says Liza's dad.
I'm sorry, everyone, but Liza won't be here for Thanksgiving dinner; her flight was delayed," says Liza's mom.
"Let us pray and thank God for this beautiful Thanksgiving meal." says her dad.

When I pick up my head from praying, my heart starts beating really fast as Liza walks in and sits down. I thought she wasn't going to make it.

"I have something that I want to say," says Liza.
"Ok, Liza; go ahead," says her dad.
"Well, I've decided that going to medical school in New York was a mistake, and I'm moving back to Florida to pursue the ministry of helping young women in need," says Liza.
"Wow, that's great, Liza, and since I work with young adults, maybe we can talk about collaborating on something," I reply.

"Thank you, Josiah. That sounds great, and I'm so grateful we're friends again," she says.
"I am too," I say as I smile.
"There's something more I want to say," Liza says as she stands up and turns toward me.
"What is it, Liza?" I ask.

Chapter 8: The Wedding

"Josiah, you're the most amazing man I have ever met. I believe you are my other half, and I don't want to live my life without you. I love you, Josiah; will you marry me?" asks Liza.

"No, Liza," I say as I get out of my seat.

"Oh, wow. I'm so embarrassed right now," Liza loudly tells herself.

"Sorry, Josiah. Forget everything I just said," says Liza as she sits back down at the table.

"Liza," I say. "I said no because I want you to know that you are the most amazing woman of God that I ever met, and you're so beautiful! I will not live my life without you because you are meant to be my wife. I want to be the one to ask you; will you marry me, Liza?" I ask on one knee.

"YES, JOSIAH. I WILL MARRY YOU!" shouts Liza as she grabs my face and kisses me.

"The courthouse will be open on Monday. We won't wait; now come here and hug me, beautiful," I say with the biggest smile.

"Congratulations!" shouts everyone in the house.

This is the best surprise of my life! Liza and I are going to be married.

Monday morning . . .

"Ok, Mr. Josiah Fernandez and Ms. Elisheba Nuñez, these are your papers; bring them back on Thursday to get married here. You do have the option to take the marriage certificate to someone legally certified to perform the wedding ceremony instead," says the clerk.

That's great! We could get married at the church instead of the courthouse.

Thursday morning . . .

My wedding day is here. With the help of our family and friends, we were able to get everything prepared in three days for our wedding.

"I now pronounce you husband and wife; you are now Mr. and Mrs. Fernandez. Congratulations!" says Pastor Hope.

"Thank you, Pastor Hope, for performing the small ceremony for us on such short notice!" says Josiah.

"I did it because you and Liza belong together. The Lord revealed it to me in a dream the night before you almost married Jael," says Pastor Hope.

"Are you serious, Pastor? How come you didn't tell me then?" I ask.

"I wanted to tell you, Josiah, but the Lord warned me not tell you because He would confirm it to you," pastor replies.

"Wow, the Lord works in mysterious ways," I say.

I'm a married man now! I married the woman of my dreams. I'm the most blessed man in the world.

Later that night . . .

"It's our wedding night, and I've waited for this moment for a long time," I say as I softly caresses Liza's forehead.

"Me too, Josiah. I'm so blessed that you're my husband!" she says.

"There's something I've waited to tell you since I met you," I explain.

"Ok, tell me, Josiah."

"One night when I was fourteen years old, I had an encounter from God. He let me know that at the age of seventeen, I would meet my future wife, but I couldn't say anything to anyone until I got married to her at age 20. I explain.

"Wow!" she exclaims.

"Liza, you were the one all along, but I couldn't tell you. At first, I tried to make it happen, but I only made things worse. When I finally let go, it happened just as God said. I will be twenty-one years old in a few days, and I didn't even remember that God said we'd be married while I'm still twenty years old until today," I say.

"That's the most amazing testimony, Josiah, just like with me having a dream about you when I was fourteen years old," says Liza.

"Let's pray together and thank the Lord JESUS for all His greatness!" I say as I get down on my knees to pray.

"Hold my hand, mama . . . *'Dear Lord God Almighty, we thank you, we love you, and we want you to be the center of our marriage. In the name of Jesus Christ, we pray, amen!'*"

Lord Jesus, you are so amazing! There is truly no God like you! You did work everything together for my good, and I'm blessed to call you my Lord and my God!

The End!

 www.ingramcontent.com/pod-product-compliance
Ingram Content Group UK Ltd.
Pitfield, Milton Keynes, MK11 3LW, UK
UKHW022223230426
12048UKWH00016BA/1033